ANIMAL STORIES

ANIMAL STORIES

By WILLIAM JOHNSTON

Designed by Walter Brooks

Illustrated by Frank Aloise and June Goldsborough

WHITMAN PUBLISHING DIVISION

Western Publishing Company, Inc.
Racine, Wisconsin

Contents

Library of Congress Catalog Card Number: 68-11118

FAMOUS
DETECTIVES
MYSTERY
STORIES

The Pig Detective

NELL PONY's yellow ribbon has been *stolen!*

Shadow the dog barked the news so loudly that Percival Pig awoke with a squeal.

"Stolen?" he exclaimed. "Goodness gracious! Well, you've certainly told the right pig!"

Percival had always wanted to be a detective. Now he saw his chance to prove that he could solve a crime.

The yellow ribbon was the ribbon that Nell Pony wore in her mane. Percival had seen it only the night before. He had been visiting Nell in her stall and had seen the yellow ribbon lying in the straw. Nell had said that it had fallen off.

Now, barked Shadow the dog, the yellow ribbon had been stolen. When Nell had awakened this morning, the ribbon was nowhere to be seen.

"The first thing a detective does is ask questions," said Percival to himself.

So, he began making the rounds of the animals in the barnyard.

First he stopped at the hen house. "Good morning, ladies," he said. "I'm not just Percival Pig this morning, I'm Percival the Pig Detective. If you don't mind, I'd like to ask you a few questions about Nell Pony's yellow ribbon."

The hens became very excited. It was the first time a detective had ever called on them.

"I saw the yellow ribbon hanging from the branch of a tree," squawked one. But then she shook her head. "Can't remember which tree," she went on. "In fact, it might have been a bush."

"I saw a horse—or maybe it was a goat or a pig—having a yellow ribbon for breakfast this morning," said another hen. "Of course, it *might* not have been a yellow ribbon. It might have been a yellow ear of corn."

That was no help. Percival was disgusted. He marched out of the hen house, paying no attention to the sudden burst of giggles behind him.

Just down the path he met two goats.

"Good morning," he said. "Did you happen to see Nell Pony's yellow ribbon hanging from the branch of a tree this morning?"

"Not me," answered the goat. "I never look up. I'm afraid that if I look up I'll see the sun falling."

The second goat said to Percival, "You should have asked *me* the question."

"All right," said Percival. "Did *you* see Nell's yellow ribbon hanging from the branch of a tree?"

The goat shook his head. "No," he replied.

Percival frowned. "Then why did you want me to ask you the question?" he inquired.

"Because my answer was better than his answer," said the second goat. " 'No' is a much better answer than being afraid of seeing the sun falling. Don't you agree?"

Percival saw that all he was going to get from the goats was more silly answers, so he waddled away. As he went, the goats suddenly began to chuckle, but Percival hurried on, hoping that soon he would solve the mystery.

"Sa-a-y, there, where are you going?" neighed the horses in the meadow behind the barn.

"I'm looking for Nell Pony's yellow ribbon," Percival replied. "Do you know anything about it?"

The horses thought for a minute. Then one of them said, "Yes, I know something about it—it's lost."

"I know that!" said Percival crossly.

"If you already know it, why are you asking us?" the second horse inquired.

"Because I'm a detective and I'm trying to find out who stole it," replied Percival. "Did you happen to see a shadowy figure slipping into the barn last night?"

"Ye-e-es," neighed the horses. "Yes, we did."

Percival was delighted. "Did you see who it was?" he asked.

"Yes, we saw who it was," replied the first horse. "It was Nell. She'd been out looking for her ribbon."

Percival groaned and waddled on. As he did, he heard laughter behind him.

"Silly horses," he grunted. And then he saw the sheep pen right ahead of him.

"Oh, dear," Percival thought. "I don't want to question the sheep. They never know *anything*."

But duty had to be done. "Hello," he said. "Have you seen Nell's yellow ribbon?"

"What's a Nell?" asked the first sheep.

"A Nell isn't a thing. Nell is the pony," replied Percival, trying to be patient.

"What's a yellow ribbon?" asked the second sheep.

For a second, Percival didn't know how to answer. "Well," he said finally, "a yellow ribbon—a yellow ribbon is a ribbon that is yellow."

"Oh, you mean Nell Pony's yellow ribbon!" said the third sheep, suddenly looking uncommonly bright for a sheep.

"Yes," said Percival. "Have you seen it?"

"Have I seen what?" replied the third sheep, not looking quite so bright anymore.

But the second sheep scowled at the third sheep and said, "Don't be a dunce! He's asking you if you've seen a yellow pony who belongs to a ribbon named Nell."

The third sheep shook her head and said, "No, I don't know any pellow nibbons named Yell." Then, puzzled, she said, "By the way, what is a pellow nibbon?"

Percival gave up and waddled away. "Baaa," said the sheep, and it sounded as if they were laughing, though Percival had never known a sheep to laugh before.

After that, Percival talked to the roosters, and then to the other pigs, and finally to the cows. Each time he got nothing but a crowing and a squealing and a mooing of silly answers—and then, as he was leaving, a crowing and a squealing and a mooing of giggles.

Sadly Percival headed for the barn to tell Nell that he had failed to find her yellow ribbon. He was very unhappy. Not only had he failed to help Nell, he had also failed to prove he could be a detective.

Nell was standing in her stall, looking almost as unhappy as Percival felt.

The instant she saw him, however, she smiled a big pony smile.

"How wonderful!" Nell cried. "You've found my ribbon! Oh, thank you!"

"Oh, no!" exclaimed Percival. "You don't understand. I can't find it at all. I–"

But at that instant, Nell lowered her head and plucked the yellow ribbon from the curl of Percival's tail.

"What a clever detective you are!" said Nell happily. "I don't know how you ever found it, but I will certainly be grateful to you forever."

For a moment, Percival didn't know how he had found it either. Then he remembered that he had visited Nell for a little while the night before. "The ribbon must have caught on my tail then," he said to himself, "and I've been carrying it around ever since."

That explained something else to Percival. Now he knew why the animals had laughed when he walked away from them. They had seen that he himself was carrying around the yellow ribbon wherever he went.

"I'm not really very clever," he told Nell Pony. And he explained how he must have picked up the ribbon by accident the night before. "You can laugh at me, too, if you want," he said bravely.

But Nell Pony didn't laugh.

"After all, Percival," she said, "it was your very first case. And you *did* find the ribbon. I'm going to hire you whenever I lose something."

Percival smiled gratefully. Maybe Nell was right. Maybe next time he really would do better. Of one thing he was absolutely certain: The next time he would look *first* at the end of his own curly tail.

The Mouse Who Found the Moon

IT ALL BEGAN when Marvin Mouse overheard Mr. and Mrs. Jones talking, and Mr. Jones claimed that the moon was made of green cheese.

Marvin returned to his nest in the kitchen wall and thought about that for a long time. If the moon were really made of green cheese, he finally decided, it would be foolish not to go there and stock up.

Marvin went to the oldest and wisest of the mice and asked him if what he had heard was true.

"Not a bit of truth to it," replied the oldest and wisest of the mice. "See for yourself. Look at the moon. Is it green?"

As it happened, the moon was shining right outside the window at that moment. Marvin looked. "No," he said, "it isn't green. It's yellow."

"And there's the proof of it," said the oldest and wisest mouse. "The moon is made of *yellow* cheese, not green cheese."

Marvin was pleased about that. He didn't think he would have cared for green cheese, anyway.

That night, Marvin announced to the other mice that he was going to visit the moon and feast on its yellow cheese.

Until then, the other mice hadn't paid much attention to the moon. Now they studied it closely.

"It's so high in the sky," said one. "How will you get there, Marvin?"

"I'll wait till it comes down," Marvin explained. "I've watched the moon, and I've seen that every night, just before dawn, it comes down to earth. It lands just behind that big hill over there."

"It will be a dangerous trip," said Marvin's cousin.

"And a worthless one," said his uncle. "There is a large box on the other side of the hill. When the moon goes down, the people put it into the box and put it away."

But nothing could change Marvin's mind. And when the moon began to go down, he headed for the big hill.

The other mice waited, telling themselves that they had seen the last of their friend. But, not long after the moon had disappeared behind the big hill, Marvin returned.

"Did you find it? Is it really cheese?" asked the others all at once.

But Marvin didn't answer. He just smiled. It was a very broad smile. Then he crawled into his nest in the kitchen wall and went to sleep.

The other mice discussed the matter. Some were sure that

Marvin had found the moon and that it was indeed made of yellow cheese. Others were just as certain that Marvin had failed.

The next night, however, when the moon began to go down, Marvin left for the big hill again. Again he returned smiling, but saying nothing.

Night after night after night, the same thing happened. And then one night one of the mice suddenly pointed at the moon and said, "Look! Look! Look at the moon!"

The other mice looked. They gasped. There was a big slice missing from the moon. It was no longer full and round, as it had been before Marvin had started making his trips.

"It's true," said one of the mice. "The moon is made of yellow cheese. And Marvin is eating it up."

"If Marvin can find it, then we can find it, too," said another of the mice.

All of the mice went marching out of the house and headed for the big hill. They walked and they walked. They came to the big hill and climbed it. But all they saw on the other side of the big hill was the other side of the big hill. The moon was nowhere in sight.

"Maybe it's a little farther," said one of the mice.

So on they marched, as far as the eye could see, and a little farther. At last they were so tired that they could march no more.

"I don't think we'll ever find it," said Marvin's cousin. "I think Marvin has it hidden."

The other mice agreed. Wearily they turned around and marched back home.

When they arrived, there was Marvin fast asleep in his nest. And, as usual, he was smiling to himself.

After that, the other mice watched crossly as Marvin left every night and came back looking contented every morning. When he was gone, they watched the moon grow smaller and smaller. In time it came to look like only half a moon.

"I know what we'll do," said Marvin's uncle. "When Marvin goes to the moon tomorrow night, we'll follow him."

And that was what they did. The next night when Marvin left the house they trailed after him. But by then the moon had become so small and, as a result, gave so little light, that they lost him in the darkness.

"Do you know what is happening?" said Marvin's uncle. "Marvin is eating all of the moon. It won't be long before there isn't any moon at all."

The mice looked out of the window. There was only one thin slice of moon left now. They knew that something had to be done and quickly, too.

When Marvin came home the next morning, all of the mice were sitting in a circle waiting for him.

"Marvin," said his uncle, "you have to stop eating the moon. If you don't, the whole world will become dark. And if the whole world becomes dark, how will we hunt for food? We need the moonlight when we go searching in the cupboards and pantry for something to eat."

Marvin smiled.

"In fact," said another mouse, "you have to put back all the cheese you've already eaten, Marvin. Look at that moon—it's only a sliver!"

"How can I put back the cheese if I've already eaten it?" asked Marvin.

That was a hard question. Not one of the mice had an answer for it.

"There is one thing I could do," said Marvin. "For the next few weeks, I want each of you to bring all of the cheese you find to me. Then I'll take it to the moon and put it back in place."

The other mice thought that was a very clever idea indeed. All the cheese they found they brought to Marvin. And every night Marvin headed for the big hill, loaded down with cheese. When he returned, of course, he no longer had the cheese with him. But he was still smiling. And he looked like the best-fed mouse in the house.

At first some of the other mice thought that Marvin might be eating their cheese instead of putting it back on the moon. But, as the weeks passed, the moon became larger and larger again. In time, it became full and round and yellow once more.

The mice were delighted, now that they had moonlight to hunt by again.

"You are very clever, Marvin," they said. "Now you must promise not to eat the moon again."

But Marvin would not promise, no matter how they scolded. In fact, he continues to this day. If you look up into the sky to-night and see that the moon is not completely round and full, you can be fairly sure that Marvin Mouse is at it again—either taking cheese away or putting it back.

Exploring

Bobby Bear, Sandy Squirrel, and Chuck Woodchuck were best friends. And three best friends sitting together under a chestnut tree should be happy. But they weren't. Not at the moment, anyway.

The trouble was, Bobby Bear and Sandy Squirrel wanted to go exploring down by the Big Pond, but Chuck Woodchuck didn't want to go.

"Come on," said Sandy Squirrel. "Maybe we'll find a nest of animal-eating jungle ants."

"The Big Pond isn't a jungle and there's no such thing as animal-eating jungle ants," said Chuck.

"Who says so?" demanded Bobby Bear.

"I say," answered Chuck. "I've been to the Big Pond a thousand times, and there's nothing there but a big pond."

"We're going exploring anyway," said Sandy. "Better come along if you don't want to miss the fun."

Chuck Woodchuck shook his head. "Who wants to explore the Big Pond?" he said. "It's always the same."

So Sandy and Bobby left Chuck at the chestnut tree and went exploring by themselves.

When they reached the Big Pond, Sandy said, "Let's explore all the way around. All the way around and back. And while we're exploring," he said, "let's pretend."

Bobby thought that was a fine idea, so off they went to circle the Big Pond.

When they had gone a little way, Sandy said, "Let's pretend it's a desert. See all the sand! And feel how hot it's getting!"

Bobby Bear began to pant and drag his feet. "Water, water, water!" he gasped. "I'm dying of thirst in this great desert!"

"Look!" Sandy shouted, pointing. "Here come the desert bandits! They're riding camels and they're going to capture us!"

"Quick! Let's hide in the mountains!" said Bobby.

The instant he said that, the desert became a mountain and he and Sandy began climbing to escape from the bandits who were chasing them on camels.

"Let's hide behind these rocks," gasped Sandy. "Maybe they won't see us here."

"There they go," said Bobby. "They're riding right by. We're safe again."

"Don't be too sure," warned Sandy. "They'll probably get an airplane and fly overhead and spot us from the sky."

"We'd better hide in the jungle," Bobby decided. "They won't be able to see us there."

And the instant he said that, the mountain became a jungle.

"The jungle's so thick, I can't see where we're going," said Sandy, clawing his way through the undergrowth of vines and brush. "I think we're lost."

"Help! Help!" Bobby called. "I've been captured by the animal-eating jungle ants! Save me! Save me!"

"I'm coming," Sandy answered. He fought his way back to Bobby and dragged him free from the ferocious animal-eating jungle ants—just in time!

"Now what'll we do?" asked Bobby.

"The only way to get out of this jungle is to find a ship and sail out," answered Sandy. He pointed again. "There's a good, stout ship," he said.

Sandy was pointing toward a big washtub which was resting at the edge of the Big Pond.

"That's the biggest, wickedest-looking ship I've ever seen," said Bobby as he and Sandy ran toward the washtub. "I'll bet it's a pirate ship. I'll bet the pirates are off somewhere in the jungle burying treasure."

"Of course it's a pirate ship," said Sandy. "Look at the big black pirate flag flying from the mast."

Bobby and Sandy hopped on board the pirate ship and pushed off.

"Look!" said Bobby. He pointed excitedly back toward the shore. "It's the pirates! They're looking for their ship! They see us!"

"They've got a cannon!" shouted Sandy. "Watch out! They're going to shoot!"

Sandy and Bobby ducked just as a cannonball whizzed over their heads and landed with a big *kerplunk* in the ocean.

"We're hit! We're sinking!" cried Bobby.

"Not yet," said Sandy. "Wait'll we get closer to shore before we're hit."

"All right," agreed Bobby. Then he pointed in the other direction, toward the middle of the ocean. "There's another pirate ship!" he shouted. "It's going to ram us!"

"Our only chance is to paddle to the other side," said Sandy.

And that was what they did. They leaned over the side, ducking cannonballs, and paddled with their paws.

When they were close to the shore, Sandy said, "*Now* we're sinking! One of the cannonballs hit us below the waterline and we're sinking fast!"

"Abandon ship!" cried Bobby.

Over the side they went. They splashed through the shallow water and scampered back to dry land.

"Whew! That was a close call," said Sandy.

"Look where we are," said Bobby. "We're right back where we started from. We've been all the way around the Big Pond."

"Let's rest awhile," said Sandy. "Then we can go exploring again."

Bobby agreed, and they went back to the chestnut tree to do their resting.

Chuck Woodchuck was still lying in the shade. "Well, what did you find—a nest of animal-eating ants?" he asked with a grin.

"Not at first," replied Sandy. "First we found a desert."

"And bandits chased us up into the mountains," said Bobby. "But we couldn't stay there because they went to get an airplane to spot us from the sky."

"So we hid in the jungle," said Sandy. "That's when we found the animal-eating ants. They captured Bobby."

"But Sandy saved me," said Bobby. "Then we found a pirate ship. But when we got out into the middle of the ocean, the pirates started firing their cannon at us from shore."

"They didn't hit us until later, though," said Sandy. "First, we were almost rammed by another pirate ship."

"Then we were sunk by a cannonball," said Bobby.

Chuck Woodchuck was staring at them. "Where did all that happen?" he asked.

"Down at the Big Pond," said Sandy.

"Pirates?" said Chuck. "And animal-eating ants? And bandits? And a desert? And you were sunk by a cannonball?"

"Look at my legs," said Sandy. "They're wet all the way up to the knees. I guess that's proof."

Chuck frowned. "I've never seen any pirates or ships or deserts down at the Big Pond," he said.

"That's because you haven't looked," said Bobby. "Some people can't see them, but that's because they don't try."

Chuck Woodchuck thought about this for a minute. Then he said, "What are you going to do now?"

"Rest," said Sandy. "Then we're going exploring again."

Chuck smiled. "This time," he said, "I think I'll go with you."

And later that day, when the three friends went exploring again, Chuck was amazed at all of the wonderful things that could be found around the edge of the Big Pond. There was a haunted house, and a submarine, and an Indian village, and more. He decided that Sandy and Bobby were right—the only reason he hadn't seen these wonderful things before was that he just hadn't looked for them.

The Cow and the Bullfighter

ONCE UPON A time in far-off Spain there was a small brown calf named Maria. One day she said to her mother, who was a large cow, "How long will it be before I will be a cow?"

"Oh, in no time at all," replied her mother.

That sounded fine to Maria. She was in a hurry to grow up.

Then she asked, "Mamma, what will I do when I become a cow like you?"

"You'll give milk," answered her mother.

"And what else?" asked Maria.

Her mother took a mouthful of grass. "That's all. You'll be a cow and you'll give milk. Why do you ask?"

Maria looked disappointed. "That isn't much," she said. "I

want to do more with my life. I want to do something *important.*"

"You listen to me, Maria," said her mother. "It just so happens that giving milk *is* important. What would people put on their cereal if we cows didn't give milk? What would boys and girls have for their birthday parties if we cows didn't give cream for ice cream?"

"Oh, I suppose giving milk is important—in a way," said Maria. "But I still want to do something else." She thought a moment, and then she said, "I know what I want to do, Mamma. I want to be a big, strong bull and huff and stamp my feet and frighten everyone for miles around."

Her mother sniffed. "Those silly bulls," she said. "All they ever do is go off to the city and fight in bullfights."

Maria beamed. "That's what *I* want to do!" she said.

Her mother was shocked. "Cows do *not* fight in bullfights," she said. "It just isn't done. It isn't ladylike."

"Then I'll be the first," said Maria determinedly. "I don't care whether it's ladylike or not. I want to do something important, and bullfighting sounds very important to me."

"Maria, I never want to hear another word about this!" said her mother. And off she went to the other side of the pasture, where the grass was thick and sweet.

Maria didn't mention bullfighting to her mother again. But she had a plan. She was determined to be the first cow ever to fight in a bullfight.

Several months later, the man came from the city to pick the bulls that looked like the best fighters. By then, Maria had grown as big as she ever would be.

So Maria went to the corral where the bulls had gathered. She watched them showing the men how very fierce and brave they were.

The bulls snorted and pawed the ground. Then they went racing, head down, toward the corral fence, as if they intended to break it to bits with their horns.

The men watched and smiled. When a bull was especially fierce, the men cheered and applauded.

"Well," said Maria to herself, "that doesn't look very hard to me. I can do that."

So she got into line behind the noisy, pawing bulls. And, in time, it came her turn to perform.

When the men saw Maria in line, they began to laugh.

"Look!" they hooted. "There is a cow who thinks she is a bull!"

Maria pretended not to hear them. She began to snort and to paw. Then she put her head down and raced toward the fence as if she intended to butt it down.

Maria acted so fierce that the men stopped laughing and cheered.

Then one of them said to the others, "I think we will take this cow to the city and put her into the bullring."

"But," said another man, "the people will only laugh when they see her there."

"True," smiled the first man. "But they will pay much money to laugh at a cow in a bullring."

That settled it.

Maria was led up onto a truck and was driven to the city to perform in the bullring.

The big day came very quickly, but not quickly enough for Maria. The animals were put into pens close to the ring. People crowded into the seats on all sides.

Then the fights began.

A bull was sent into the ring. Standing in the center of the ring was a man holding a red cape.

When the bull saw the cape, he went charging at it, snorting, head down, and tried to butt it with his horns. But when he reached the man, the man lifted the red cape out of the way, and the bull charged noisily by.

This happened time and time again. Finally, it seemed the man grew tired of the game. He pulled out his sword and hid it behind the red cape. This time when the bull charged at the red cape, the man held out the sword instead. The bull went plunging right into it.

"Oh, dear," Maria said to herself. "How could the bull make such a foolish mistake? He must have known that the man was going to pull the cape out of the way. He must have known that sooner or later he was going to run into that sword. If *that* is all there is to bullfighting, I have traveled a very long way for nothing!"

At last it was Maria's turn to fight. A man made an announcement to the crowd, telling them that this was the first time in the history of bullfighting that a cow had ever appeared in the bullring.

The crowd laughed. They thought it was funny.

The gate of Maria's pen was opened, and Maria trotted out into the ring.

"Fight! Fight!" roared the crowd.

Maria intended to do just that. But she certainly wasn't going to do it the same way that the bulls had.

Maria put her head down, all right. And she went charging toward the man with the red cape.

But when she reached the man, she did a very surprising thing. She stopped and bellowed.

The man was so surprised that he nearly tumbled over backward.

Maria bellowed again.

The crowd roared with laughter again. But now they were laughing at the man with the red cape. He looked as if he hadn't the slightest idea what to do about a cow who bellowed at him at the top of her voice.

The man became very, very angry. "Fight, you cow!" he cried. "Fight like a bull!"

Maria just bellowed louder.

"Look at the brave bullfighter," laughed the crowd. "He is afraid of a cow!"

That made the man so angry that he threw down his cape and pulled out his sword.

"Now, you cow!" he snarled at Maria. "I will slice you up into meat loaf!"

And he probably would have, too, if Maria had fought him like a bull. But Maria was a lady, and she fought like a lady.

Instead of charging the man in the usual way, she turned and

she kicked. She kicked the sword right out of his hand.

"Hurrah! Cheers for Maria!" shouted the crowd. And they laughed until they could laugh no more.

As for Maria, she simply trotted back to her pen. It was quite clear to her and to everyone else that she had won.

That day could have been the beginning of a great career for Maria as a fighter. But it wasn't, for she refused to go into the ring anymore. At last the men sent her back to the farm.

"I was wrong about bullfighting," Maria explained to her mother. "It isn't important—it's just silly. What is really important in this life is giving milk so that children can have it with their cereal and can have ice cream for their birthday parties."

Maria's mother might have said, "I told you so." But she didn't. She just nodded her head and led Maria to a far corner where grew the sweetest, greenest grass in all the meadow.

Arnold and Mr. Pastuli

Arnold was a middle-aged horse. Like most middle-aged horses he had a number of aches and pains, and his bones stuck out a little more than they had when he was younger. But Arnold didn't fret about his aches or the way he looked. He was much too busy to care about the fact that he was not the youngest, handsomest horse in the world.

Arnold pulled the wagon for Mr. Pastuli, the scissors-grinder man. Every morning, except Sunday, he and Mr. Pastuli would start on their rounds. It was usually late evening before they returned. There was very little time to be sad, and if ever Arnold did begin to feel sorry for himself, there were many children to cheer him up.

When Arnold and Mr. Pastuli entered a street, the bell clanging, all the children ran out to greet them. And then, while Mr. Pastuli ground the knives and scissors for the mothers, the children played with Arnold, talked to him, and brought him tasty lumps of sugar.

When the children played with Arnold, they pretended he was some sort of horse other than a scissors-grinder's horse. Sometimes they pretended he was a circus horse. They would trim his mane with bright ribbons, and then they would call out, "Prance, Arnold!"

And Arnold would prance as well as he could. He would lift one front foot, then the other front foot, snort a bit, and make believe that he was prancing beautifully. If he did any more than that, he would be reminded of his aches and pains.

Other times, the children played Wild West. They pretended that Mr. Pastuli's wagon was a covered wagon, and that a whole tribe of ferocious Indians were attacking. They would dart about, pointing their fingers and shouting, "P-*kew*—P-*kew*—P-*kew!*" Then they would take cover not only behind the wagon but also behind Arnold.

Arnold enjoyed his life with Mr. Pastuli. Pulling the wagon wasn't much of a chore; it was a very light wagon even with Mr. Pastuli perched on the seat. And he liked playing with the children and listening to the women gossip while they waited for their knives and scissors to be sharpened. So, the day that Mr. McAlister came to talk to Mr. Pastuli was a very sad day for Arnold.

Mr. McAlister was a salesman who sold trucks. He brought a bright new yellow truck with him the day he called on Mr. Pastuli.

"Look at that truck!" Mr. McAlister said. "Isn't she a beauty?"

"Is she a she?" Mr. Pastuli said. "How can you tell?"

"All trucks are she's," Mr. McAlister explained. "And this little beauty, Mr. Pastuli, is ready to go to work for you right now!"

"What could she do for me?" Mr. Pastuli asked, puzzled. "I already have someone to cook my meals for me."

"I'm talking about your grinding," Mr. McAlister said.

Mr. Pastuli looked doubtfully at the truck. "I don't think she could do my grinding for me," he said. "It takes special talent and years of study."

"No, no," Mr. McAlister said. "I mean this little beauty can carry your grinding equipment around for you."

"But I have Arnold and my wagon to do that for me," Mr. Pastuli said.

"And how many miles a day can Arnold cover?" Mr. McAlister asked. "No matter what the number is," he went on, "this little beauty can do twice that. Let's say, Mr. Pastuli, that now you are able to sharpen a hundred knives a day. With this little beauty working for you, you would be able to sharpen two hundred, maybe three hundred, knives a day. You would make two or perhaps three times as much money."

Mr. Pastuli shook his head. "I have more money now than I need," he said. "I have so much money, I'm running out of socks."

"Excuse me," said Mr. McAlister. He couldn't believe he had heard right. "You're running out of socks?"

"That's where I keep my money," Mr. Pastuli explained. "My socks are so full of money, I have trouble finding an empty pair to wear."

"Then let me put it another way," said Mr. McAlister. "Don't you think it's about time you put Arnold out to pasture? Look at him! If he took two steps without resting, he'd fall down and never be able to get up again. Mr. Pastuli, Arnold deserves a rest!"

Arnold snorted youthfully so that Mr. Pastuli would think he was still full of the old pepper. But it was such an effort that it brought on a coughing spell.

"Maybe you're right," Mr. Pastuli said sadly to Mr. McAlister. "Come into the house and we'll talk about it."

Not long after that, Arnold lost his job. He was driven in a large truck to a farm, and Mr. Pastuli came along to say good-bye and make sure his old friend was comfortable.

"This will be a wonderful life for you, Arnold," Mr. Pastuli said. "No more work. No more pulling a wagon. You can graze in the pasture all day, without a worry or care in the world."

Arnold sighed. It sounded pleasant, but he wished he could tell Mr. Pastuli that the old life had been plenty good enough.

Every morning after that Arnold went directly to the pasture to graze. He ate the sweet green grass for a while, and then he just stood around and thought. He thought about his aches, and then about his pains. He began to be disturbed by the fact that he was not the youngest, handsomest horse in the world. Most of all, he thought about the children and wondered what exciting games they were playing now.

Arnold became miserable. He complained all the time. He complained about his stiff back, and he complained about the fact that there weren't any strawberries in the meadow—even though he had never in his whole life had a strawberry. Arnold became so grouchy and gloomy that none of the other horses on the farm wanted to be anywhere near him.

Then one day Mr. Pastuli came back.

"Hello, Arnold," he said. "How do you like it here on the farm?"

Arnold snorted.

"Well, to tell you the truth, that's the way I feel about it, too," Mr. Pastuli said. "That truck didn't work out so well. When I drove it down the street, nobody paid any attention. Nobody brought any scissors or knives to be sharpened. It seems that, in this day and age, trucks are not very unusual. Nobody notices a truck. But a horse—now *that's* something different!"

Arnold snorted again—very happily this time.

So now Arnold is back pulling Mr. Pastuli's wagon. And Mr. Pastuli's business is as good as it ever was. When he and the wagon and Arnold enter a street, ringing the bell, all the children run out to meet them. And not far behind them are the mothers, telling each other the news as they bring knives and scissors to be sharpened.

Arnold, of course, is so busy pulling the wagon from neighborhood to neighborhood and playing with the children that he has completely forgotten about his aches and pains. He doesn't care a bit that he isn't the youngest, handsomest horse in the world. In fact, he doesn't even think about it.

Albert's Adventure

"THE TROUBLE IS," said Albert Zebra for the nine hundred and ninety-ninth time, "nothing exciting ever happens in the jungle."

Sometimes he said it to himself. Sometimes he said it to the other animals. Sometimes he even tried to get them to do something about it.

For instance, when he came upon a group of monkeys who were playing leapfrog, he would say, "Why don't you play by the bank of the river? Then the one who leaps over will land in the water."

"That may be exciting," the monkeys would reply, "but it's

also dangerous. We can't swim."

"Pooh-pooh!" Albert Zebra would exclaim. "Who's afraid of danger?"

One day, as he was strolling along the jungle path, Albert came upon an elephant and a leopard who were in the midst of a terrible argument. The leopard claimed that he had been asleep and that the elephant had awakened him by walking too heavily. The elephant retorted that he had just as much right to walk heavily as the leopard had to sleep.

In time, the argument ended in the same way that many arguments end, with the leopard and the elephant stomping off angrily, each of them convinced that he was right.

"What a wonderful chance to start an exciting battle between

the elephants and the leopards," said Albert to himself. "I can be a spy," he went on. "In fact, I can be a double spy. I can spy on the elephants for the leopards, and I can spy on the leopards for the elephants."

The only problem was that both the elephants and the leopards knew that Albert was always trying to cause a little excitement. He knew that they wouldn't pay any attention to him if he tried to start a battle between them.

"I'll have to disguise myself," Albert decided. So he trotted off to the Big Mud Hole and rolled in the mud. When he came out, his white stripes were the same color as his black stripes. Albert no longer looked like a black-and-white-striped zebra. He looked just like a black-all-over horse.

Disguised in this way, Albert went off in search of the leopard family. He found them napping in their favorite clearing.

Albert awakened the leopards. "I happened to be passing by the elephants a few minutes ago," he said, "and I heard them say that all leopards have tails that look like snakes."

Of course, the leopards didn't recognize Albert. They thought he was a black horse. And when they heard what he said, they became very angry indeed at the elephants.

"I'll tie those elephants' trunks in knots," snarled one.

"I'll drop coconuts on their heads," roared another.

Albert Zebra was quite pleased with the excitement he had caused. He volunteered to help the leopards by being their spy, and the leopards agreed.

Next, Albert went in search of the elephants. He found them resting in the high grass.

"I just happened to be passing by the leopards a few minutes ago," he said to the elephants, "and I heard them say that all elephants have big ears."

That was true, of course. Elephants *do* have big ears. But, because the elephants thought that the leopards had said it, they became very angry.

"I'll pull their tails with my trunk," bellowed one.

"I'll toss them all as high as the tallest tree in the jungle," threatened another.

Albert fairly jumped with excitement. Then he offered to help the elephants by spying on the leopards, and the elephants quickly agreed.

So Albert galloped back to the leopards.

"I've been spying on the elephants for you," he said, "and what do you think? I think they are going to build a leopard trap. And when all the leopards are caught in it, they're going to dump it in the river!"

The leopards were furious. Immediately they started talking about building an elephant trap, and when all the elephants were caught in it, pushing it off a cliff.

So Albert dashed back to the elephants.

"I've been spying on the leopards for you," he said, "and what do you think? The leopards are getting ready to attack!"

The elephants flopped their ears.

"We'll attack them first!" they trumpeted. They chose one elephant to be their general and he began lining them up to march on the leopards.

Albert Zebra dashed back to the leopards.

"The elephants are marching! The elephants are marching!" Albert shrieked.

"We're ready for them!" the leopards growled. Then they chose one of their number to be their general, and he began lining them up to fight off the elephant attack.

Stuffed right up to the ears with excitement, Albert Zebra pranced to one end—the far end—of the clearing to wait for the battle to begin.

It wasn't long before the elephants appeared, trumpeting fiercely. They lined up on one side of the clearing, facing the leopards who were on the other side and who were growling and snarling savagely.

Then the elephant general called across the clearing. "We're

going to chase you leopards right out of the jungle!" he bellowed.

"Ho-ho!" answered the leopard general. "We leopards are going to take you elephants by the tails and pull you inside out!"

"Is that so!" said the elephant general. "We elephants are going to stretch your whiskers and tie them in bows!"

"Indeed?" snarled the leopard general. "We leopards are going to take you elephants apart and put you back together again with your tails in front and your trunks in back!"

That went on for hours. The leopards shouted across the clearing at the elephants, and the elephants shouted back across the clearing at the leopards. And Albert Zebra grew more and more pleased with all the excitement he had caused.

Meanwhile, something else was happening. First the sky clouded over. Then it began to drizzle. Then it began to sprinkle. And finally it began to rain.

After it had been raining for a few minutes, the elephant general happened to glance over in Albert's direction. And what do you think? The rain had washed Albert clean. He no longer looked like a black-all-over horse. He looked like a black-and-white-striped zebra.

"Look at our spy!" said the elephant general. "He isn't a spy at all—he's Albert!"

"*Your* spy!" said the leopard general. "He isn't your spy, he's *our* spy!" But then he looked at Albert, too. And he changed his mind. "He isn't a spy at all," he said. "He's Albert!"

It didn't take the leopards and elephants long to figure out what had happened. When they did understand it all, they stopped being angry at each other. Instead, they became angry at Albert.

"Stay where you are!" they snarled and bellowed. "We're coming after you!" But Albert was already racing down the path.

They chased him through the jungle, trumpeting and growling as they ran. They chased Albert so far that it took him a month and a day to find his way back.

After that, Albert was a changed zebra. He no longer went around trying to make things more exciting. "After all," he told his own children many years later, when they asked for a story, "being chased by a pack of elephants and leopards is enough excitement to last a zebra a lifetime."

A Whale of a Fish Story

"Now WHAT should we do?" asked Chuck Woodchuck. He and Bobby Bear and Billy Beaver had played every single game they knew how to play.

Since they were near the Bear family cave, Bobby Bear said, "Let's ask my mother what we can do."

But when they asked Mrs. Bear, she suggested that they take a nap.

"Oh, *Mom,*" said Bobby.

"What *else* can we do?" asked Chuck.

"Let's ask my father," said Bobby. "He might have a better idea."

"Why don't you go fishing?" said Mr. Bear when they asked

him. "When I was a cub and couldn't think of anything else to do, that's what I did."

The boys looked at each other.

"We've never been fishing," said Bobby to his father. "How is it done?"

"Simplest thing in the world," said Mr. Bear. "You just trot down to the Big Pond and climb out on the Big Log, and when a fish swims by, you catch it. You have to be fast, though. For some reason or other, the fish don't care to be caught."

Going fishing sounded like fun, so Bobby and Billy and Chuck started off for the Big Pond.

On the way, Billy said, "I think I'll catch a catfish. I can keep it as a pet."

"I'll catch a dogfish, and it can chase your catfish up a tree," laughed Chuck.

"I think I'll catch a whale," said Bobby.

Chuck and Billy stopped short. Bobby stopped, too.

"A whale?" said Chuck, a little uneasily. "Do you really think there might be a whale in the Big Pond?"

Billy Beaver took a step backward. "If there *is* a whale in the Big Pond," he said, "I don't think I really care much about going fishing."

Bobby was sorry that he had even thought about catching a whale. He had never seen a whale, but he had heard stories, and he knew that whales were the very biggest of all the big fish.

"Listen," he said, trying to be brave, "what are we worried about? If there were a whale in the Big Pond, somebody would have noticed it—I think."

That sounded right to Billy and Chuck. And so, eager once more, the three continued on their way to the Big Pond.

When they got there, they did exactly what Bobby's father had told them to do. Very carefully, they crawled out onto the Big Log.

"I don't see any fish," said Chuck, peering down into the water. "All I see is the bottom of the pond."

"Maybe they don't know we're here," said Billy. "Let's make a lot of noise. Then they'll hear us and come swimming up so we can catch them."

That sounded like a sensible thing to do. So they began shouting at the tops of their voices.

Bobby Bear shouted, "HALLOOOOOOOOOOOO! HALLOOOOOOO! HALLOOOOOO!"

Billy Beaver shouted, "WABBA! WABBA! WABBA! WABBA! WABBA!"

Chuck Woodchuck shouted, "FISHY-FISHY-FISHY-FISHY-FISHY!"

But not a single fish appeared.

"I think we're scaring the fish away," said Bobby. "Remember? My father said that, for some reason, they don't care to be caught."

"We'd better be *very* quiet, then," said Billy Beaver, "so the fish won't know we're here."

Pretty soon they spotted a fish. It wasn't a very big fish. But it was swimming along lazily, making funny fish faces to itself, and it was headed straight for the Big Log.

"I'll get it," whispered Bobby.

"No, I'll get it," whispered Billy. "It's closer to me."

"It's coming right to me—I'll get it," whispered Chuck.

Just then, the little fish reached the log. And at the same moment, Billy and Bobby and Chuck plunged their paws into the water to catch it.

All three of them caught something—but it wasn't the little fish. Billy caught Bobby's paw, Bobby caught Chuck's paw, and Chuck caught Billy's paw.

As for the little fish, it swam off, waggling its tail, without a care in the world.

"We'll have to take turns," said Bobby. "Billy, you catch the first fish, and, Chuck, you catch the second fish, and I'll take the last fish."

That seemed fair, so they settled down to wait again.

Before very long, a middle-sized fish came swimming toward the Big Log.

Billy Beaver, who had the first turn, got ready to plunge his paw into the pond.

"That fish doesn't look very friendly," said Chuck Woodchuck.

"In fact, he looks very unfriendly," muttered Bobby Bear. "I'm glad it's not my turn."

By then, the fish had reached the log.

"Now!" shouted Chuck.

Billy Beaver plunged his paw into the water. But he had become so upset by the unfriendly look of the fish, and by Chuck's shout, that he plunged too far. And—*splash!*—into the pond he tumbled.

Of course, he missed the fish. Down he went under the Big Log and popped up on the other side.

"Look! A beaverfish!" shouted Chuck Woodchuck. He was too excited to realize that there was no such thing as a beaverfish. He just shouted, "My turn!" and plunged his paw into the pond after Billy Beaver.

Naturally, Chuck missed, too. *Splash!* Into the pond he went.

Bobby Bear looked at the two heads bobbing about in the pond, the beaver head and the woodchuck head. He shook his own head in disgust. "I guess it's *my* turn!" he said. He offered one paw to Billy and the other paw to Chuck—and fished out one beaver and one woodchuck.

While Billy and Chuck were drying off in the sun, Billy said, "I don't know why we were so worried about catching a whale. Why, we couldn't catch a whale if it jumped out of the pond and dropped into our laps."

Billy chuckled to himself, but when he looked at Bobby and Chuck, they weren't laughing at all. Instead, they were staring past him, with their mouths hanging open and their eyes nearly popping out.

Billy turned around and looked, too.

What he saw was the most gigantic, wide-open mouth imaginable. As he stared, the wide-open mouth seemed to open wider and wider—as wide as a hole, then as wide as the doorway to a cave, and then almost as wide as the whole pond. And all the while it was moving slowly along the water toward the Big Log.

"The whale!" Billy shrieked. "It's the whale!"

And that was exactly what Bobby and Chuck were thinking.

At once, all three of the fishermen turned tail and scampered off that log. They ran through the woods as fast as their twelve legs would take them. And they didn't stop until they reached the Bear family cave, where they fell into a heap, panting and still looking almost as frightened as when they had first spotted that gigantic, wide-open mouth.

Just then, Mr. Bear came out of the cave. "If you're looking for fish around here," he smiled, "you won't have much luck."

Billy and Bobby and Chuck all started talking at once, telling Mr. Bear about the whale. They talked so fast that Mr. Bear had a hard time understanding them, but eventually he was able to make out what they were saying.

"A whale, eh?" he said, smiling a different kind of smile. He looked as if he did not believe them.

"It *was* a whale!" Bobby insisted. "We saw its mouth—wide open! It was as big as the whole pond!"

"Even bigger!" said Billy. "As big as a lake!"

"Even bigger than that!" said Chuck. "It was as big as an ocean!"

"Well," said Mr. Bear, smiling that smile again, "I think I'd like to see a whale as big as that—a whale as big as an ocean that could fit in a pond. Come along," he said. "Let's take a look."

Bobby and Billy and Chuck followed Mr. Bear as he headed for the Big Pond. They covered their eyes with their paws and peeked out just enough to see where they were going.

When they reached the pond, Mr. Bear said, "Now then, where is that—"

He stopped. Then he began to laugh. He laughed so hard that tears came to his eyes. He laughed so hard that he had to sit down to keep from falling down. He laughed so hard that he had to curl up into a ball and hold his sides.

Billy and Bobby and Chuck could not understand what was so funny. For, when they peeked out from behind their paws, there was the wide-open mouth of the whale, just as they had seen it before. Except that now it did not look quite as large. Not quite as large as an ocean, or a lake, or a pond. In fact, it wasn't even as large as Mr. Bear.

Mr. Bear finally stopped laughing. "I'm afraid your whale isn't a whale after all," he said. "If you'll look a little more closely, you'll find that it's really an old washtub that someone has thrown into the pond."

The three fishermen looked more closely. Indeed, it was an old washtub. It still looked like a wide-open mouth, but it didn't look very large anymore.

Then Mr. Bear said, "I can't promise that you'll catch a whale, but if you're still interested in fishing, I'll show you how it's done."

Billy and Bobby and Chuck agreed that they wanted to learn. So Mr. Bear led them out onto the Big Log. He taught them how to sit very quietly until a fish came along. Then he taught them how to plunge a paw into the water and catch the fish against the log—instead of grabbing at the fish and frightening it away.

It wasn't very long before the three friends had caught so many fish that, taken all together, they probably would have weighed nearly as much as a whale.

"Let's have a fish picnic," suggested Bobby Bear.

"Let's," said Chuck and Billy.

And so that was what they did, and they all had a whale of a good time.

The Dog-Eating Whatchamacallit!

BOZO WAS A small, sad terrier who lived in a big city. He did not have a home of his own, and so he spent his days trotting about the streets, looking for scraps of food. At night he slept wherever he could find shelter.

One summer day, Bozo was walking down the street, wondering where he could find something for dinner, when, *whop!*—he found himself caught fast in the dogcatcher's strong net.

"Oh, dear!" Bozo moaned to himself. "This is surely the end of me!"

The dogcatcher's truck rattled down the street to the pound, and Bozo was put into a large pen with many other dogs.

"I'll probably have to spend the rest of my life here," he

thought. He was so accustomed to having bad things happen to him that he always expected the very worst to happen.

The next day, Bozo saw many people gathered outside the pen. They pointed at one dog and then another, and some of them called or whistled. As each dog was pointed out, the keeper took him out of the pen and gave him to someone in the crowd.

"Oh, woe is me!" Bozo thought. "Something terrible is happening to these poor dogs. And I'll be next!"

He crouched in a far corner of the pen, hoping no one would see him and point at him.

But, on the third day, someone did see him, and someone did point at him. That someone was a little boy who stood close to the pen, a little girl and a big man right behind him.

The keeper pulled Bozo out of the pen and handed him to the little boy.

"We're going to take him to our farm," said the big man. "Hope he'll like it."

Bozo didn't know what a farm was, but he guessed that it must be a horrible place.

"Help!" he barked to the other dogs in the pen. "Help me!"

But, to his dismay, no one came to his rescue.

"When you get to the farm, watch out for the dog-eating whatchamacallit!" barked one of the older dogs who liked to tease.

Bozo didn't know whether to believe him or not.

As they drove out of the city, the little girl held Bozo on her lap and petted him. "Good dog," she whispered.

But Bozo knew it was only a trick. The reason she was holding him, he guessed, was to keep him from escaping.

The farther from the city they traveled, the more worried Bozo became. There were no tall buildings in the country. There was no noisy traffic. It was so *quiet!* He shivered and hid his head under his paw.

At last the car stopped. Bozo looked out the window and saw a large white house. He saw another large building—this one red—and several smaller buildings. He supposed that the smaller buildings were where all the poor dogs were kept penned up.

When the boy opened the car door, Bozo leaped out of the little girl's lap and ran. He darted across the yard and dived under the porch of the house.

The man and the boy and the girl came over to the porch. They bent down and called to him. But Bozo remained crouched in the darkness.

"Come out. Please come out," the little girl begged. "If you do, I'll show you the farm."

Bozo knew what that meant! She would probably feed him to the dog-eating whatchamacallit!

The boy went into the house and brought out a big bone.

"Look," he called. "Look at what I have for you."

But Bozo did not move.

Finally, he heard the man say, "I think he's frightened, poor fellow. Let's not bother him. When he makes up his mind to it, he'll come out on his own."

Then the man and the children went into the house.

After they had gone, Bozo poked his nose out from under the porch and looked around. Near the big red building he saw many strange-looking animals, the like of which he had never seen before. Then, lying on the doorstep in the sun, he saw a fat, green-eyed cat.

"Another trick," he said to himself. The man and the children must have guessed that Bozo liked to chase cats. They had left the cat there to draw Bozo out of his hiding place.

"You're wasting your time," he said to the cat. "I'm not going to chase you."

The cat purred contentedly. "I'm glad to hear that," she said. "When I heard my master talking about getting a dog, I thought there might be trouble."

Bozo scowled. Was it possible that the cat was not a trick after all?

"Where is the dog-eating whatchamacallit?" he barked.

The cat stretched in the sun. "I don't think we have one on this farm," she purred lazily. "But, then, I'm not positive. I spend most of my time here on the doorstep in the sun."

Bozo nodded toward the strange-looking animals across the yard. "What are those?" he asked. "Could one of them be a dog-eating whatchamacallit?"

The cat looked back over her shoulder toward the big red building. She laughed a small, purry laugh. "That one is a pig, and that one is a horse, and that one is a chicken," she said.

Bozo didn't know what to believe. He pulled in his nose and crouched in the darkness under the porch to think.

"Well," he decided after a while, "I can't stay under this porch forever. And I don't know the way back to the city. The only thing to do is find that dog-eating whatchamacallit and find out how fierce it is!"

Trembling, he slipped out from under the porch and went running across the yard toward the big red building. As he did so, the animal that the cat had called a chicken went clucking and fluttering out of his way.

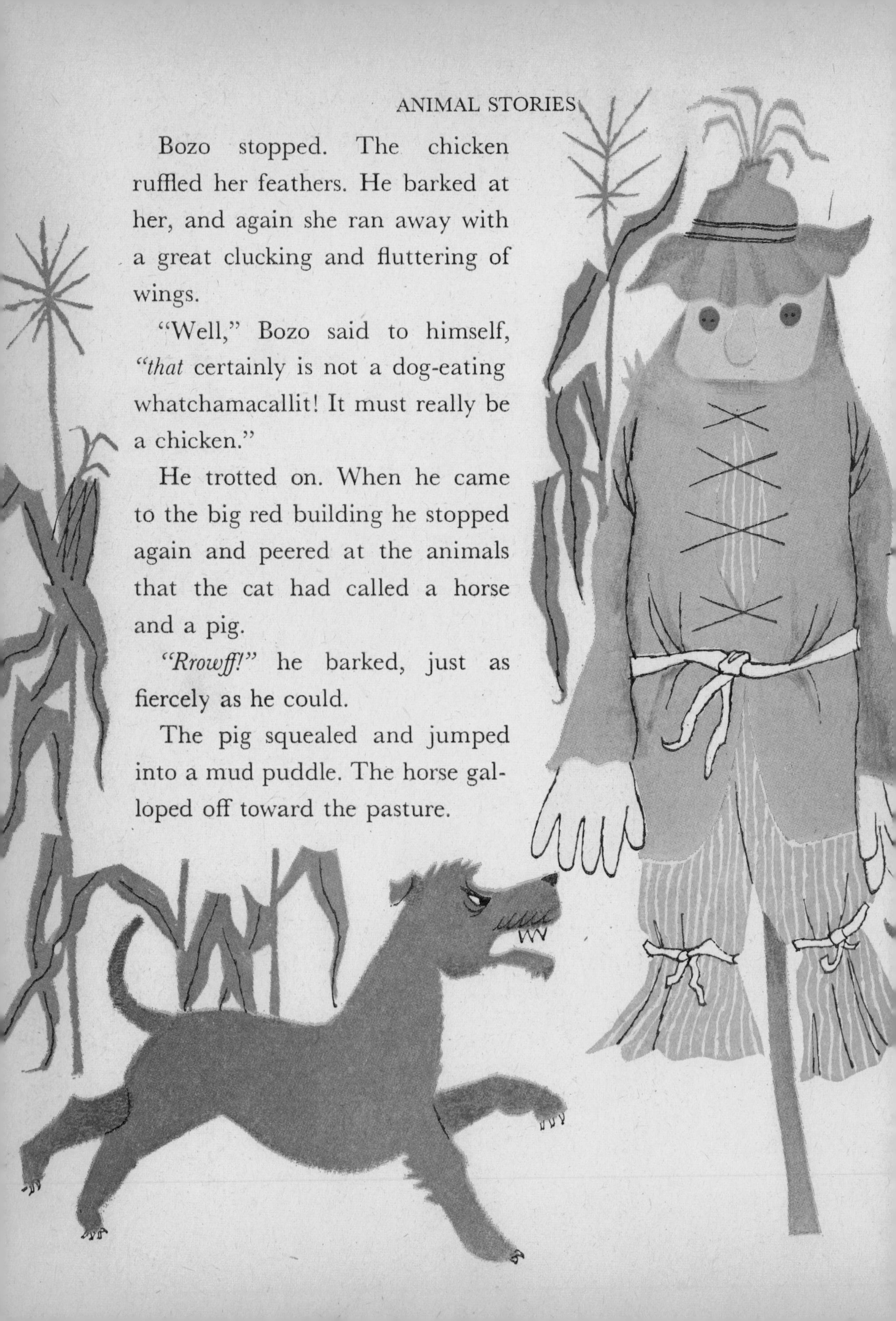

Bozo stopped. The chicken ruffled her feathers. He barked at her, and again she ran away with a great clucking and fluttering of wings.

"Well," Bozo said to himself, "*that* certainly is not a dog-eating whatchamacallit! It must really be a chicken."

He trotted on. When he came to the big red building he stopped again and peered at the animals that the cat had called a horse and a pig.

"Rrowff!" he barked, just as fiercely as he could.

The pig squealed and jumped into a mud puddle. The horse galloped off toward the pasture.

Bozo was delighted. He pranced around the farmyard, barking and leaping and having a wonderful time. "A farm isn't so bad," he said to himself. "Maybe there is no such thing as a dog-eating whatchamacallit!"

But at that very moment a frightening sight loomed in front of him. He had wandered near the cornfield, and close to the edge of it stood what looked like a very tall man. It was dressed in torn and tattered old clothes, and it had long arms that looked as if they would grab any dog who came near.

"Rowf!" barked Bozo. "It's the dog-eating whatchamacallit!" He turned to run and then he stopped. He didn't want to go back under the porch and hide in the dark again. He loved the big, bright farmyard.

"Be brave!" he told himself fiercely. And suddenly—he was!

With a growl, he leaped at the tall, ragged figure and tore it to pieces. Surprisingly, it was easy to do. The whatchamacallit didn't even try to fight back.

Bozo trotted proudly across the yard. This time, instead of hiding under the porch, he went to the back door and barked.

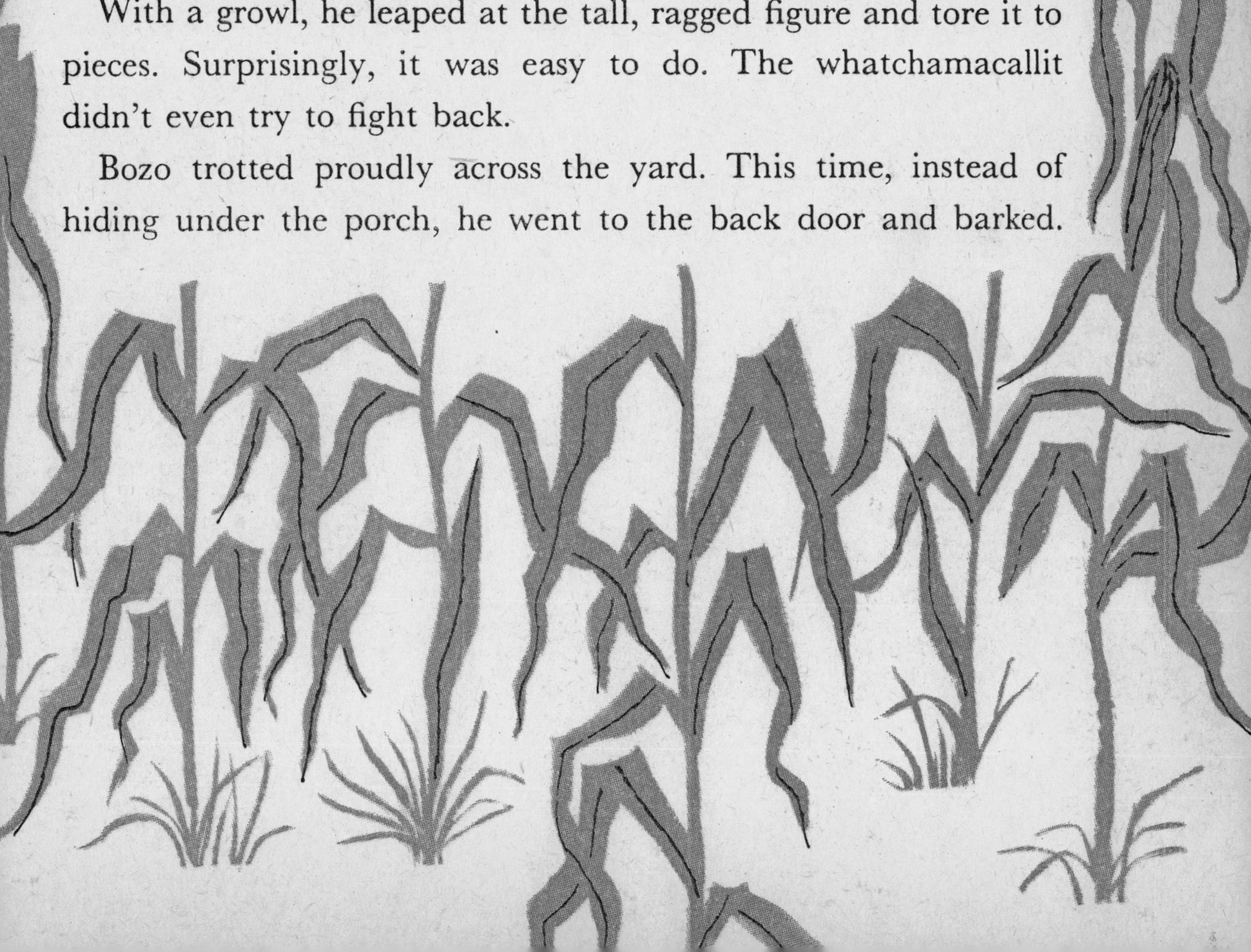

Soon the man and the two children came out.

The little girl snatched Bozo up in her arms and hugged him. The little boy said he was going to begin that very evening to teach Bozo how to bring in the cows.

"You'd better teach him about scarecrows, too," the man said, smiling. He pointed toward the cornfield. "Look at the mess he made of that one. It's ripped to ribbons!"

The children looked and laughed. Bozo wondered if he had done something foolish. Still, he thought, he didn't *feel* foolish. He felt brave. He had fought the dog-eating whatchamacallit, and he had won the right to stay on the farm. It looked as if something good was going to happen to him after all.

The Horse in the Spare Room

SOCRATES AND DILBERT were cats. Socrates was a thin cat and Dilbert was very round. They were pets in the home of Mr. and Mrs. Hollywhistle.

One afternoon when Socrates was dozing in the sun on the window seat, Dilbert hopped up and lay down beside him and said, "What is black and white and red and has four legs?"

"How should I know?" muttered Socrates grumpily. He didn't like being awakened to answer a riddle. "What *is* black and white and red and has four legs?"

"A horse," replied Dilbert.

Socrates opened one eye. "A horse!" he exclaimed. "Who ever saw a red, white, and black horse?"

"I did—just now," answered Dilbert. "There's a red, white, and black horse in the extra bedroom."

Socrates opened the other eye. "Who said it was a horse?" he asked.

"Mr. Hollywhistle said so," replied Dilbert. "He told Mrs. Hollywhistle that he put the horse for the new baby in the spare room. And I looked. And there it was."

"I'll have to see that before I believe it," said Socrates, getting up. "Show me. I'll bet it isn't a horse."

Dilbert led the way to the bedroom.

"Now, where is that horse?" asked Socrates, peering nervously around the door.

"There," whispered Dilbert.

Then Socrates saw it. It was a horse, all right. It was a white horse, with a black mane and a red saddle.

"Great buckets of cream!" said Socrates.

"Shhhhh!" cautioned Dilbert. "You'll wake it! It's asleep!"

Socrates lowered his voice. "Let's get out of here!" he said. "It might wake up and chase us!"

Socrates and Dilbert scampered back to their window seat.

"A horse in the house is dangerous," said Socrates. "When I was a kitten, I was very nearly stepped on by a horse."

"But he looks like rather a nice horse to me," said Dilbert. "He sleeps all the time."

"You won't think he's such a nice horse when he wakes up and steps on your tail," said Socrates. "And you won't like it when he learns to do tricks and the Hollywhistles decide that it's more fun to have a tricky horse than two sleepy cats around the house."

Dilbert began to worry. "You're right," he said. "There's just not room enough in this house for a tricky horse and two sleepy cats. That horse must go!"

"Who's going to tell him?" said Socrates.

"Not me," said Dilbert quickly. "I don't want him to step on *my* tail!"

"I'm not going to, either," said Socrates. "So I guess we'll just have to show him that we're trickier than he is. We'll have to trick him out of the house."

"How?" asked Dilbert.

"We'll do something naughty and see that he gets blamed for it," replied Socrates. "Then the Hollywhistles will send him back where he came from."

"But what can we do that we can blame on a horse?" said Dilbert. "We can't scratch the table legs—the Hollywhistles know that horses don't have claws. We can't swing on the curtains—it takes claws to do that, too."

"Let's see," said Socrates, thinking. "What do horses do?"

"They pull wagons," Dilbert said.

Socrates shook his head. "That's no help."

"They run races," Dilbert said.

Socrates thought about that for a moment. Then he shook his head again and said, "No, that won't do, either."

"They eat grass," Dilbert said.

Socrates brightened. "A-ha!" he said. "A-ho! That's it! Mr. Hollywhistle is very proud of his lawn. If he thinks that horse has eaten all the grass, he'll send him galloping quickly enough!"

"There's just one thing wrong," said Dilbert. "Who's going to eat the grass so Mr. Hollywhistle will think that the horse ate it up?"

"We are," Socrates said.

Dilbert groaned. "Cats don't eat grass," he said.

"How do you know? Have you ever eaten any?" said Socrates.

Dilbert shook his head. "No."

"Then if you haven't eaten any, you don't really know whether cats eat grass or not," Socrates said. "Let's go."

Dilbert and Socrates slipped out of the house. When they reached the front lawn, Dilbert looked at the green grass and said, "It doesn't look much like milk."

"Don't be foolish!" said Socrates. "It must be healthful. Horses eat it, and look how big horses get."

Dilbert swallowed hard. Then he took a nibble of grass. "Hummmm, it isn't so bad," he said, chewing.

So Socrates took a nibble, too. "I suppose if we *had* to eat it we might even get to like it," he said.

They continued to nibble at the grass—but, though they ate for a long time, only a small patch of grass disappeared. And both

Socrates and Dilbert began to feel rather strange.

"You're looking a bit green around the eyes," said Dilbert to his friend.

"I feel green all over," moaned Socrates. He started to drag himself toward the house. "I think I'll leave some grass for tomorrow . . . or maybe the next day," he said weakly. "I've had enough for one meal."

Dilbert wandered after him. "I don't think I'll be interested in grass again until I can have some milk on it," he said.

Feeling quite odd, Dilbert and Socrates stretched out on the windowsill.

Not long after that, Mr. Hollywhistle came home from the office, and Mrs. Hollywhistle met him at the door.

"Have you looked at the lawn lately?" asked Mr. Hollywhistle, looking puzzled. "Something has been nibbling the grass."

Mrs. Hollywhistle laughed. "I'd say it was that horse you brought home for the baby," she said, "except that I've never heard of a merry-go-round horse that could eat grass."

From the windowsill came a sad moan.

When Mr. and Mrs. Hollywhistle had gone on to the kitchen, Dilbert looked at Socrates and said, "A merry-go-round horse! It isn't a *real* horse. It's a merry-go-round horse!"

Socrates sighed with relief. He almost smiled. "We're saved!" he said. "There's nothing to worry about now."

"I don't see why," said Dilbert. "We still have a horse in the house."

"But a merry-go-round horse!" said Socrates. "Just as a merry-go-round horse does not eat grass, a merry-go-round horse does not step on cats' tails."

"I see what you mean," said Dilbert happily. "I feel better, too."

And both cats put their heads down and had a long, contented snooze in the warm sun.

The Student King

When little Leander, the lion cub, was born, all the animals were pleased to see that he looked exactly like his father, good King Leo.

"If he is like his father," they said happily, "then he will be strong and brave and wise. When he grows up and takes his father's place, he will be a very fine king."

King Leo was the most pleased of all. "I'll start right now to teach him how to be king," he said to Leander's mother.

"Isn't it a little too soon?" she replied. "He's only a cub."

"It's never too soon," said King Leo. "Why, when I was his age, I was already known as the strongest, bravest, wisest cub in the jungle."

So, that very day, King Leo took little Leander out into the jungle to teach him how to be king.

"First," said King Leo, when they had reached a clearing in the jungle, "you have to be very strong. I usually show how strong I am by wrestling with a gorilla. But a gorilla might be too big for you to handle at your age. You can start right now with a monkey."

"How shall I do it?" asked Leander.

"We'll wait here," said King Leo. "When a monkey comes along, you pop out and challenge him to wrestle. Then you leap on him and pin his shoulders to the ground, and hold him there until he cries 'uncle,' which means he gives up."

That seemed easy enough to Leander. He hid beneath a bush, and when he saw a monkey come along the path, looking for jungle berries, he popped out and said, "I challenge you to wrestle!"

"I don't want to right now," said the monkey. "I'm hunting berries."

Leander hesitated. That seemed like a much better idea than wrestling. "I'll help you," he said finally, and he and the monkey began hunting berries together.

King Leo sighed. Then he snatched little Leander away and took him to another part of the jungle.

"If you're going to be a king, you must keep your mind on what you're doing," King Leo said crossly. "What kind of a king would I be if every time I went out to wrestle a gorilla I ended up picking berries?"

"You'd be a berry-picking king," replied Leander.

King Leo sighed again. "We'll try wrestling some other time," he said. "Right now, I'll teach you how to be brave. You see," he went on, "I show how brave I am by frightening away hunters. We'll wait right here, and when a hunter comes along, I want you to jump out and roar your loudest roar to frighten him away."

That seemed simple enough to Leander. When a hunter came down the path, carrying a big net, Leander leaped out and roared his loudest roar, looking as ferocious as he possibly could.

But, since he was only a cub, Leander was unable to look very frightening. And his loudest roar was only about as loud as an automobile horn—which did not frighten the hunter in the least.

The hunter grinned at Leander. Then he began to laugh. "Come here, little fellow," he called, and he waggled a finger at Leander, motioning him toward the net.

Leander thought the hunter wanted to play a game. He began frisking about, making happy purring sounds—and getting nearer the net every second.

Fortunately, King Leo realized that the hunter was not just playing a game. He wanted to trap Leander in the net. Out leaped King Leo, and he roared his loudest roar! It was so loud that it sounded like a thousand thunderstorms.

The hunter nearly jumped out of his boots. He dropped the net and went scooting back toward his camp without looking back over his shoulder even once.

King Leo was quite annoyed. "What kind of a king would I be," he said to Leander, "if every time I went out to frighten a hunter I ended up playing games?"

"You'd be—" Leander began.

But his father shushed him. "Maybe I can teach you to be wise," said King Leo. "Let's go back to our cave."

When they reached the cave, Herman Hippopotamus was waiting outside. He had come to get some advice from the king.

Good King Leo invited Herman into the cave and asked him what his problem was.

"Well, my mudhole has dried up," replied Herman. "I can no longer take baths."

King Leo turned to Leander. "What would you advise him to do?" he said.

Leander thought a minute. Then he answered, "I think he ought to dig up the mudhole and move it down to the river."

King Leo sighed again. "It's impossible to dig up a hole," he explained to Leander. "The more you dig, the bigger the hole gets."

Then King Leo told Herman Hippopotamus to ask one of his elephant friends to carry some water from the river in his trunk and squirt it into the mudhole. In that way, the hole would become wet again.

As soon as Herman Hippopotamus had gone, King Leo said to Leander, "I think I'm the one who needs some advice. I've been teaching you all morning, and you still aren't strong or brave or wise. The only thing to do is to ask *my* father how he taught me to be a king."

So King Leo and Leander left their cave and went to the cave where Leo's father lived. His name was Lancelot, and he had been king before Leo.

When they got there, King Leo explained the problem to his father. "I've spent the whole morning trying to teach Leander how to be a good ruler," he said, "but he's still not strong or brave or wise. I don't understand it," he said, shaking his head in dismay. "He looks like me. Why isn't he strong and brave and wise, the way I am?"

Lancelot Lion smiled. "Leander *is* exactly like you—exactly the way you were when you were a cub," he said. "I remember when you were his age. I took you out to teach you how to be a king. But instead of learning to wrestle, you went off chasing a butterfly. Instead of frightening a hunter, you almost got caught in his net. And when Elmer Elephant came to my cave one day to ask how to keep from stepping on the end of his trunk, you advised him to try tying his trunk to his tail."

When he heard this, King Leo smiled, too. "I'd forgotten that day," he said.

Then, turning to Leander, King Leo said, "I guess it's a little too soon to teach you how to be a king. We'll wait until you're bigger to teach you to be strong, and until you're older to teach you to be brave and wise. As for right now," he said, "you can go out and play."

Leander went romping happily off. As he ran down the path he felt quite proud, for he knew he had learned at least one thing that day. He had learned that before a lion becomes a king, he must have some time to be a cub.

"I'll remember that when I have a cub of my own," he thought. And then he saw some big, juicy jungle berries, and they looked so good that he forgot everything else and hurried to pick them.

Corky the Sea-Going Mouse

CORKY WAS A city mouse. He lived with his father and mother and a great many other mice down by the docks in a warehouse. From the warehouse Corky could see ships from all over the world.

The one thing Corky wanted most of all to be was a seagoing mouse. He wanted to go to sea and see all the marvelous sights of the world that his Uncle Roger had told him about.

Corky's Uncle Roger had been a sailor when he was young. He had spent a long time at sea, sailing from country to country aboard the big ocean liners. He had had wonderful adventures.

But whenever Corky told his mother he wanted to go to sea, she said, "When you're old enough, dear."

And whenever Corky told his father he wanted to go to sea, he said, "Fine. Good idea—but not yet."

Corky was getting very tired of waiting. So one day, when he was feeling very grown-up, he decided to run away and go to sea.

On his way, he stopped to see Uncle Roger, who was nibbling some grain in a corner of the warehouse. "Uncle Roger," he said, "when I go to sea, what should I know?"

Uncle Roger thought a minute, twiddling his whiskers. Then he answered, "There are two rules that a mouse ought to follow when he goes to sea. The first is: Always keep one eye on your tail. The other is: Always keep the other eye on the passengers."

"On my tail?" said Corky, puzzled.

"Yes," replied his uncle, "because if you don't keep one eye on your tail you're liable to find the ship's cat with his paws on it. And that's very bad luck. The favorite snack of ship's cats is ship's mice."

Corky trembled. "I promise," he said. "I'll keep one eye on my tail." Then he said, "But, Uncle Roger, why should I keep the other eye on the passengers?"

"Because," answered Uncle Roger, "when you see the passengers leaving the ship, that means it's sinking. It's always a sure sign."

Corky shivered. Still, he wanted to go to sea. Down to the docks he scampered, and, because he did not know very much about ships, he slipped aboard the very first ship he saw.

Getting aboard was not difficult. There was a wide walkway connecting the ship and the dock. A great many people were crossing the walkway, so Corky simply scurried aboard between their feet.

Once on board, he hid himself in a coil of rope. From there he could see what was going on, but he could not be seen by the passengers.

Soon there was a loud *clang!* The gate to the walkway closed. Then there was an even louder *toot,* and the ship began to move away from the dock.

Corky was absolutely delighted! At last! He was going to sea!

The ship rolled gently as it got under way.

Corky looked around. Right in the middle of the deck was a sandwich stand. Many of the passengers were gathered around it, buying sandwiches and ice cream and soda.

"A-ha! A-ho!" said Corky to himself. "That's where I'll eat. After dark when the sandwich stand is closed, I'll slip in there and have a feast."

But the thought of food made Corky feel very odd. The gentle rolling of the ship made him feel worse.

Corky groaned. "Oh . . . oh-oh-oh . . . oh-wo-wo-wo-wo." He hoped it would not be long before the ship reached a foreign country so he could get off and rest for a while.

Suddenly there was a sharp *bump,* and the ship shivered from stem to stern. Corky was so frightened that he forgot about feeling sick. He looked out and saw all the passengers leaving the ship.

Corky remembered what his uncle had told him—that when the passengers leave the ship it is sinking. He leaped out of his hiding place and scampered toward the walkway.

But he found to his dismay that he was too late!

The passengers had all left, and now—to Corky's great surprise—other passengers were coming aboard.

Corky shouted at them. "Stop! Stop!" he shouted. "Go back! Go back! The ship is sinking!"

But they paid no attention, of course. For even when a mouse shouts, it sounds like a squeak.

The passengers kept coming. Finally Corky had to scramble back to his hiding place to keep from getting trampled.

Then there was a loud *clang* again, as the gate closed, and a louder *toot,* as the ship began to move.

Corky sighed. He decided that the sailors must have been able to repair the ship, so he settled down inside the coil of rope once more.

Unfortunately, with all the excitement going on, Corky forgot to keep one eye on his tail. He was just getting comfortable when he heard a familiar hiss—a cat sound. When he looked around, he saw the ship's cat, a big gray puss with yellow eyes, about to pounce on him.

Corky sprang from his hiding place just in time. Between the passengers' feet he raced, under their seats, along the railing—with the ship's cat right behind him every step of the way.

Lady passengers screamed. Little boys joined the chase. Sailors began swatting at Corky with brooms. Corky was certain he would not get away.

Then, just as the cat was about to seize him, Corky felt the sharp *bump* again. This time he knew what it was. And he knew what to do. He raced toward the walkway, with the cat and the sailors and the little boys still at his tail.

Corky got there first. He reached the walkway and dashed across it—onto the dock. It was a sad thought, to be landing on a foreign shore, perhaps never to see home again, but it was better than being caught by the ship's cat.

"Corky! Stop!" a familiar voice was calling.

Corky looked around in amazement. Who could possibly know his name in this foreign country? To his astonishment, not ten steps away stood Uncle Roger.

"What's happened, Corky?" asked Uncle Roger. "You look frightened."

All in one breath, Corky told his uncle about running away and going to sea, about the strange feeling he had at sea, about the ship sinking—but not sinking—and about the ship's cat.

Uncle Roger laughed. He laughed so hard that Corky thought he would never stop.

At last he said, "You weren't on a seagoing ship, Corky. You were on a ferryboat. The ferry carries people from one side of the river to the other." Then he added, "The ferry wasn't sinking,

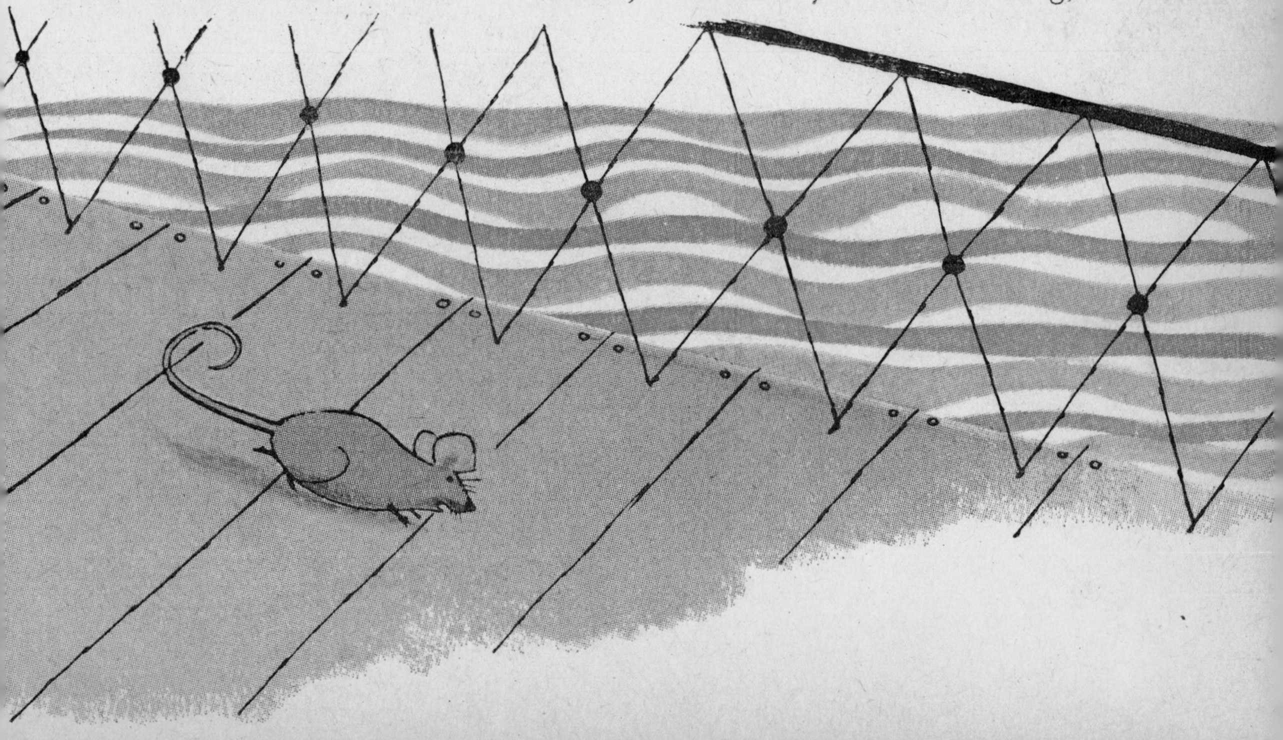

Corky. It was just letting passengers off on the other side of the river—and picking up new passengers to bring them to this side of the river."

"Well, I *thought* it was sinking," said Corky grumpily, "and that's *almost* the same."

Uncle Roger laughed again. "The next time you decide to go to sea," he said, "let me know about it and I'll show you a real oceangoing ship."

"I'll do that," said Corky.

But he never did. Because he had decided that if he ever had a hankering to see the world again, he would just look out the warehouse window.

The Treasure Hunt

IT WAS THE first day of spring. The air smelled like all the flowers in the world. Sandy Squirrel and his two best friends, Bobby Bear and Chuck Woodchuck, were lying under a chestnut tree feeling extremely lazy. They felt so lazy, in fact, that they didn't even snap at the pesky butterfly that kept fluttering back and forth under their noses.

"We ought to get up right now and do something," sighed Sandy Squirrel.

"Why?" asked Chuck Woodchuck drowsily.

"Because," answered Sandy, "it's a doing-things day. And the next time it rains and we have to stay indoors, we'll wish we'd done something today when the sun was shining."

"We *are* doing something," said Bobby Bear. "We're lying under this tree."

"I mean something fun," said Sandy. "Like hunting for treasure."

"There's no treasure around here," said Chuck. "If there were, the grown-ups would have found it by now."

"I don't think they've ever looked," said Bobby Bear. "Have you ever seen any grown-ups around here looking for treasure? I haven't."

Sandy Squirrel leaped up, frightening the pesky butterfly, who went flying off to find a safer place in which to play.

"Let's look!" said Sandy excitedly. "If we find treasure, we'll be rich!"

Bobby Bear jumped up, too, as eager as Sandy was to go treasure hunting.

But Chuck Woodchuck just chuckled and closed his eyes. "There's no treasure around here," he said again. "If you'll excuse me, I'll just do a little daydreaming instead."

That was how Chuck Woodchuck happened to be left behind when Sandy and Bobby started out to hunt treasure.

Using their paws, they began digging behind the tree in which the Squirrel family lived.

They did turn up a number of things. They found an old shoestring. And they found the root of a bush—which pulled a trick on them by suddenly breaking as they were tugging it and tumbling them backwards down the Big Hill, almost to the edge of the Big Pond. They also found seven rusty soda bottle caps, and a number of worms who burrowed deeper into the ground.

But no real treasure was to be found.

"I think Chuck Woodchuck was right," said Bobby Bear wearily. "There's no treasure around here."

Sandy was just about to agree with him, when suddenly, near the tree, he spotted something small and brown and round. He picked it up.

"A nut!" he announced happily as Bobby Bear came running up.

Bobby was excited, too, because, to squirrels and bears, nuts are very valuable.

"Still," said Bobby after a moment, "one nut doesn't make a treasure."

"No," said Sandy, "but two is a start." And he pointed to another nut lying on the ground not far away.

"Come on!" said Bobby. "I think we're on the trail of the biggest treasure ever!"

Sandy and Bobby went scampering along, finding one nut after another. And then—they came to a familiar-looking pair of feet. When they raised their eyes, they found Sandy Squirrel's father peering down at them.

"What are you two chasing?" Mr. Squirrel asked.

"We're on the trail of treasure," explained Sandy. "Look! We've already found all these nuts!"

Mr. Squirrel was puzzled. "That looks like a little more than luck," he said. Then he recognized the nuts, and he said, "I'm sorry, boys, but I was taking some nuts out of winter storage this morning, and I guess I must have dropped these few that you have found."

Disappointed, Sandy and Bobby handed over the nuts. Then they went back to digging.

"I *thought* that was too easy. You never find treasure on *top* of the ground," said Bobby.

Sandy stopped digging. "Of course!" he said. "It wouldn't be lying around on top of the ground, and it wouldn't be buried here, either. Both places are too easy. We have to look in a hard place."

"Where?" asked Bobby.

"In the hollow log where my mother and father keep things," answered Sandy. "My mother says that once she puts a thing

away, she can never find it. So the hollow log must be the hardest place in the world in which to find things."

Sandy and Bobby hurried off to the hollow log. But when they crawled inside they weren't so sure they wanted to be there, for the log was dark and damp and a little bit frightening.

"Where shall we look?" asked Bobby, a shiver in his voice.

"In all the darkest corners," answered Sandy. "I know that's where I'd hide a treasure if I were hiding a treasure."

So they began tiptoeing around—although they didn't know exactly *why* they were tiptoeing—peeking and poking into all of the darkest places in the hollow log.

They found a number of things. They found a collection of last year's oak leaves, which Sandy's mother had put away to use later as between-meal snacks. And they found an old string, which Sandy's father had saved because he said you never could tell when an old string might come in handy.

Then they found something—in fact, a number of things—that were round and shiny.

"It's the treasure!" cried Sandy.

"But what are they?" asked Bobby. "I can't see in here."

"They're round and shiny—they must be jewels!" said Sandy. "Let's take them out into the light!"

Sandy and Bobby were so excited that they very nearly tripped over their own feet getting out of the hollow log. As they came tumbling out they bumped into Sandy's older brother, Samuel.

"Hey!" said Samuel, surprised. "Where are you boys going with my marble collection? I was just going to get it."

"Marbles!" said Sandy and Bobby together.

They looked at the round, shiny things and saw that Samuel was right. They weren't jewels at all; they were marbles.

Samuel laughed. Then, taking the marbles, he explained. "I collect them when the boys lose them," he said. Then he handed one of the marbles to Sandy and one to Bobby. "That's for bringing them out of the hollow log for me," he said. "It's your reward."

Just then, Sandy's mother came down from the Squirrel family tree. "Who's been doing all this digging?" she said.

Sandy and Bobby looked a little sheepish. "We have," they said.

"Well, you did a very good job of it," said Sandy's mother. "I wanted this space cleaned up and cleared of all the rusty pop bottle caps and roots." Then she said, "I'm going to give each of you a reward. Is a blueberry enough?"

"Yes!" shouted Sandy and Bobby delightedly.

Just as Sandy's mother disappeared up the tree to get the blueberries, Sandy's father appeared.

"There you are," he said, speaking to Sandy and Bobby. "I've been looking for you. It seems to me that you deserve a reward for finding all those nuts for me." He gave one nut to Sandy and one nut to Bobby.

"Thank you, Father," said Sandy.

"Thank you, Mr. Squirrel," said Bobby.

After Sandy and Bobby had received their blueberries from Sandy's mother, they went skipping off to the chestnut tree where they had left Chuck Woodchuck daydreaming. He was still at it.

"Who says there's no treasure around here!" said Sandy and Bobby, showing Chuck their blueberries and nuts and marbles.

For a second, Chuck Woodchuck just stared, amazed. Then he leaped up, right out of his daydreaming, and ran off down the path.

"Where are you going?" Sandy called after him, laughing.

"To start digging!" Chuck shouted back. "I'm going to hunt treasure!"

The Extremely Noisy Goose

No ONE IN the barnyard ever forgot the day Carlotta Goose was atched.

"Good morning," she said, stepping out into the golden sun-hine. And everyone leaped into the air, startled beyond words. For Carlotta's voice sounded like ten trumpets, six trombones, and eleven saxophones, all off-key, and all blaring at once!

Mrs. Goose, Carlotta's mother, was the most startled of all. She ran to a nearby haystack and dived into it. A moment later she very cautiously poked her head out to see what had made that wful racket.

There were no trumpets in sight—no trombones and no saxo-hones. Only Carlotta.

"Was that you, dear?" asked Mrs. Goose.

"Yes, Mother," replied Carlotta. This time her voice was like four hundred tin cans rolling down a tin roof.

Mrs. Goose shuddered. "Speak a little more softly, dear," she said to Carlotta.

"Yes, Mother," answered Carlotta, sounding like a dozen fire sirens. Even though Carlotta wanted to speak more softly, she couldn't do it. She had only one voice, and each time she used it, it made more noise than the time before.

As Carlotta grew older—and her voice grew louder—Mrs. Goose began plugging up her ears with kernels of corn. That kept her from hearing the terrible sound of Carlotta's voice, but it also kept her from hearing everything else. Holding a conversation with Mrs. Goose became very difficult.

Peter Pig, for instance, might ask her what she thought of the pleasant weather.

And she would answer that she didn't think it was possible fo[r] a pig to grow feathers.

Or Tom Turkey might comment that lately the farmer wh[o] owned the farm was getting more milk from the cows.

And Mrs. Goose would reply that he was certainly a silly farm-er if he thought he could get silk from a plow.

Or Randolph Goat would say that it looked like rain.

And Mrs. Goose would run to get out of the way of the train.

The other animals in the farmyard did not care to plug up their ears with corn, since they wanted to hear what was going o[n] in the world. As a result, nearly every day some unpleasant acci-dent occurred.

One day, when Peter Pig was standing at his trough drinking milk, Carlotta strolled by and said, "Good morning, Peter."

It sounded like an empty bucket falling down a flight of steps.

Peter Pig was so taken by surprise that he leaped right into the trough of milk.

Another time, when Randolph Goat was nibbling the paper label from a tin can, Carlotta came passing by and said, "Nice day today, isn't it, Randolph?"

It sounded like six hundred cooking pots falling down an empty well.

Randolph was so startled that he swallowed the tin can whole.

What was even worse was that Carlotta talked in her sleep. The animals would go to bed and in a few minutes they would all be snoring away quite contentedly. Then, along about midnight, Carlotta, who was just as sound asleep as all the rest, would think of something to say.

No matter what she said, of course, it sounded like something else—like someone beating on a tin lid with a hammer, or like fifty automobiles caught in a traffic jam and tooting their horns.

Finally, Peter Pig called a meeting and said that something had to be done about Carlotta and her voice.

"I have a suggestion," said Randolph Goat. "In fact, two suggestions. First, I suggest that Carlotta sleep outside from now on so we can all get some rest. Second, I suggest that she not speak to anyone unless she is spoken to. That way," he explained, "if none of us speaks to her, she'll have no excuse for talking."

The other animals agreed that Randolph's ideas were just what were needed.

Carlotta was not very happy about the rules. She thought they were unfair. After all, it wasn't really her fault that she had a very loud voice. It was the only voice she had, and there was nothing she could do about it.

But she was an agreeable goose, and she didn't want to lose her friends by telling them they were treating her unkindly. So she nodded her head to show that she would do as they asked.

Life was not very pleasant for Carlotta after that. She slept outside the barn, all by herself. None of the other animals—except her mother, of course—ever spoke to her. She thought for a while of moving to another farmyard, but she didn't do it. She knew she would have to take her voice along with her, and the animals at the new farm would undoubtedly be just as disturbed by the noise as were her friends here.

One night, a very mysterious thing happened. When the animals awakened, they noticed that Henrietta Chicken was missing. They didn't worry at first; but, that night, when Henrietta was still missing, they began to worry about her.

The next morning, not only was Henrietta still missing, but Tommy Duck was gone, too.

Once more, Peter Pig called a meeting. "I think I know what has happened," he said sadly. "The wicked fox is slipping into the barn at night after we've gone to sleep!"

The animals clucked and neighed and mooed and grunted in dismay.

"What shall we do?" they asked each other. "Oh, what shall we do? Who will be next?"

In time, Peter Pig quieted them. "We'll have to post a sentry," he said. "Someone must stay awake at night and watch for the fox. Who will do it?"

"I will," replied Mrs. Chicken bravely. "I want to help, and, besides, it is very easy for me to stay awake."

And so that night Mrs. Chicken roosted beside the feeding trough, outside the barn, not far from where Carlotta was accustomed to sleep. Mrs. Chicken was to cry out and warn the others if she saw the fox.

Carlotta decided to stay awake, too. She hoped that Mrs. Chicken would get lonely and want someone to talk to. But, as it turned out, Mrs. Chicken did not remain awake long enough to get lonely.

As Carlotta watched—silently—she saw Mrs. Chicken's eyelids start to droop. She saw her friend's head begin to nod, and a moment later Mrs. Chicken was sound asleep.

Carlotta tucked her own head

under her wing, preparing to go to sleep, too. But just then she heard a sound. When she looked out, she saw the wicked fox creeping quietly toward the feeding trough. In the moonlight she could see a hungry glint in his eyes. And he was heading straight for Mrs. Chicken!

Carlotta wanted to cry out a warning. But she remembered the rule that she was not to speak unless she was spoken to. So she remained silent, trembling, while the wicked fox crept closer and closer to Mrs. Chicken.

Then the fox saw Carlotta. He stopped. "Ho, ho!" he exclaimed. "Answer me, goose. Who is fatter, you or this chicken?"

Carlotta cleared her throat. Now that the fox had spoken to her, she was sure it was all right to speak.

"HELP!" she cried. "FOX IN THE FARMYARD!" She shouted just as loudly as she could.

Well, when Carlotta shouted, it was a noise like none that had ever been heard in the barnyard before. It sounded like ten trumpets, six trombones, eleven saxophones, four hundred tin cans rolling down a tin roof, a dozen fire sirens, an empty bucket falling down a flight of steps, six hundred cooking pots tumbling

into an empty well, a hammer beating on a tin lid, and fifty automobiles caught in a traffic jam and tooting their horns—all at once.

The shout awakened not only Mrs. Chicken and the other animals, but also the farmer, his wife, and all the other people for miles around.

And the fox? Well, the fox was so frightened by the noise that he very nearly turned inside out trying to get away!

The next morning the farm animals had another meeting.

"I have two suggestions," said Randolph Goat. "First, I suggest that Carlotta Goose move back into the barn to sleep. I'm sure her talk won't bother *me.* Second, I suggest that Carlotta be allowed to speak whenever she pleases. In fact, I hope she talks all day long."

"Hurrah!" shouted the animals. "Say something, Carlotta!"

After that, the sound of Carlotta's voice could be heard any hour of the day or night in the farmyard. No one ever again told her to stop talking. And no one ever saw the fox again, either.

Brutus the Bike-Riding Bear

Brutus was not the smartest bear in the world. On the other hand, he was not the dullest bear in the world. He was somewhere in between. There were days when he was so clever that he caught more fish and found more berries than any other bear in the forest. There were other days when he was not clever at all, and on *those* days he couldn't walk around a tree without getting completely lost.

Brutus was very proud of himself because he had never been captured by the circus men. Other bears had been caught, but each time the circus men came looking for performers, Brutus had always been in another part of the forest.

"I am really quite clever about *that,*" he said to himself.

But one day Brutus saw an odd-looking box with a bunch of berries hanging inside it at the far end.

"That looks interesting to a clever bear like me," said Brutus.

He stepped into the box and instantly there was a loud *bang* behind him. The door of the contraption had slammed shut! Brutus did not have to think very hard to realize that the box was a trap—and he was in it!

Before very long a half-dozen men appeared. They carried the trap—with Brutus in it—to their truck. Then they drove toward the town. Soon Brutus saw a great number of tents up ahead. He knew then that he was being taken to the circus.

The men who had captured Brutus put him into a cage. To his left, in another cage, was a tired-looking old lion. In the cage to his right was a laughing hyena.

"Welcome," growled the lion. "You must be the new bicycle-riding bear."

"I don't think so," replied Brutus. "I've never ridden a bicycle in my life."

"Har! Har! Har!" laughed the laughing hyena.

"Oh, you'll learn," said the lion, speaking to Brutus. "Max, the animal trainer, will teach you."

The following day, Brutus found that the lion was right. Max, the animal trainer, was a large man with a large moustache and shiny black leather boots. He came to the cage and looked in at Brutus.

"Very good," said Max, after a minute. "You'll make a fine bicycle-riding bear."

Then he put a leash around Brutus's neck and led him into the largest of the big tents. In the center ring was a two-wheeled bicycle fitted with two smaller training wheels.

"Now, bear," said Max, "you'll have your first lesson. Hop up on the seat and do a couple of turns around the ring. Don't be afraid. The training wheels will keep you from falling."

Brutus looked at the bicycle. He looked at Max.

"I don't want to be a bicycle-riding bear," he thought to himself. "I want to be back in the forest where I can do what I want to do when I want to do it. I am *not* going to learn to ride the bicycle."

Perhaps, he thought, if he refused to learn, Max would send him home to the forest.

"All right, bear," said Max. "Let's not waste any more time. Hop up on the seat."

Brutus pretended that he did not understand. Instead of hopping up onto the seat of the bicycle, he stood on his head.

"No! No! No!" cried Max, pulling angrily at his large moustache. "On the seat! Not on your head!"

Brutus pretended to misunderstand again. This time he rolled over twice and then leaped to his feet and did a little dance.

Max jumped up and down angrily in his black leather boots and told Brutus he was undoubtedly the silliest bear in captivity. Then he took Brutus back to the cage.

When Max had gone, Brutus told the tired old lion and the laughing hyena about his plan. "A few more times like that," he said, "and Max will send me straight back to the forest."

"Har! Har! Har!" laughed the hyena.

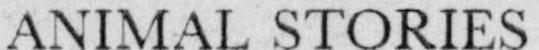

"Why is he laughing?" Brutus asked the lion.

"Perhaps because all he ever does is laugh," replied the lion. "Or perhaps he's laughing at your plan."

"But why should he laugh at my plan?" asked Brutus. "I think it is very clever myself."

"Well," answered the lion, "he knows that standing on your head, and rolling over twice, and doing little dances are not the way to get back to the forest. Max will think about it for a while, and then he will make you a circus star, anyway. You will become famous as the bear who rolls over twice, stands on his head, and does little dances."

"All right, if that's the way it is, then I won't do those things," said Brutus. "Instead, I'll sulk here in this cage and look very, very mean. Will that get me sent back to the forest?"

"Oh, no!" replied the lion. "Then you will become famous as the most ferocious bear in captivity."

"Oh, my," sighed Brutus. "What *shall* I do?"

"Well," replied the lion, looking suddenly wise as well as tired, "if I were a bear who didn't want to be a bicycle-riding bear, what I would do is learn to ride a bicycle."

That, of course, didn't make any sense at all—that is, until Brutus had given it a great deal of thought. Then, when he understood, he grinned from ear to ear and laughed—har! har! har! —like a laughing hyena.

The next day, when Max took Brutus to the big tent to teach him to ride the bicycle, he got the surprise of his life. Brutus didn't hesitate a second. He hopped right up on the bicycle and began pedaling merrily around the ring.

Max was delighted. He said that if Brutus kept it up he would soon be the best bicycle-riding bear in the business.

And that's about the way it worked out. Within a few days, Brutus was riding without the help of the training wheels. In a week he had learned to ride while standing on his head on the seat. Then he learned to ride backward and blindfolded. And every day he went faster and faster.

Finally the day came when Brutus was to make his first appearance as a star of the circus. The big tent filled with people. The performance began. Around the ring paraded the animals. Then the stars began their acts—the trapeze artists, the lion tamer, the clowns, the dancing elephants.

At last the ringmaster stepped into the center ring and announced: "Ladies and gentlemen of all ages! The Greatest Circus

in the World proudly presents Brutus the Bike-riding Bear!"

The trumpets trumpeted. Then Brutus appeared, pedaling his bicycle as fast as he could make it go!

A cheer went up! But almost immediately it turned into a gasp of surprise. Because Brutus did not stop at the center ring. He went whizzing right past it—and right out the other side of the tent! On he went, through the circus grounds, right out the exit, and across the town, pedaling for all he was worth!

Brutus did not slow down until he had reached the edge of the forest. Then he rested his bicycle against the trees, where Max, the animal trainer, could find it, and away he ran into the forest.

When he was safe again, in his favorite cool, dark cave, he allowed himself one long laugh—har! har! har!—hyena style. Because, with the help of the lion, he had just pulled off the cleverest trick of his life!

The Lapdog

WHO IS THIS?" barked Figaro the puppy one bright sunny morning. He was looking up at a tall lady with a pretty smile who had come to his box in the kitchen to admire him.

"That is the Lady of the House," replied his mother. "When she is near, you must act like a little gentleman."

"May I bark?" asked Figaro.

"No," his mother replied. "I want the Lady of the House to like you. Someday, when you are older, you may become her lapdog."

"What does that mean?" Figaro asked, puzzled. "Am I supposed to sit on my lap? I don't think I will ever be able to do it."

His mother laughed. "Silly pup," she said. "It means that

someday the Lady of the House may allow you to sit on *her* lap. You will stay in the parlor with her when she receives guests, and you will ride in her carriage when she goes into the city, just as I do. But first you must learn to be a gentleman. When she puts you on her lap, she will expect you to sit very quietly."

That didn't sound like much fun to Figaro. "Do I have to be a lapdog?" he asked.

"It's a great honor," replied his mother.

"Why is it an honor?" asked Figaro.

"Because," his mother answered. "Just because. Some dogs are yard dogs and some dogs are lapdogs, and lapdogs are better thought of."

"What's a yard dog?" asked Figaro.

But his mother had tired of questions and had gone to see whether dinner was nearly ready.

It wasn't long, however, before Figaro found out what a yard dog was. He was in the kitchen when he heard excited barking. He looked out the window and saw a number of dogs having a wonderful time as they chased each other around, snapping and yipping and barking and rolling in the leaves.

"Those must be yard dogs," Figaro said to himself. And the second he said it, he knew he wanted to join them.

Very quietly he slipped out through a little door in the big door—the little door that was meant for dogs—and then he went racing out into the yard.

The yard dogs were quite friendly. They invited Figaro to play their game with them. The game was called Catching Leaves. It was played by bounding about the yard, yipping and yapping, trying to catch as many leaves as possible.

Almost every day after that, Figaro slipped out secretly and played with the yard dogs. They became very close friends. In between times, he learned how to be a lapdog. Every morning his mother had him lie very quietly with his nose between his front paws.

"Don't move a muscle," she would say.

"Can't I even wag my tail?" asked Figaro.

"A little gentleman does *not* wag his tail!" his mother replied.

Figaro sighed sadly. He had no wish to be a lapdog.

As time passed, the weather changed. The leaves were raked away. Then the snow fell.

Figaro learned a new game from his friends in the yard. It was called Catching Snow. The dogs raced around the yard, yipping and yapping, trying to catch as much snow as they could.

It was a fine game, but Figaro couldn't spend much time playing it. His mother had begun making him sit still for longer periods.

"Any day now, the Lady of the House will invite you to sit on her lap, Figaro," she said. "You must be ready."

Then the snow melted, and it was spring. Figaro spent every morning practicing to be a lapdog. But in the afternoon, while his mother was with the Lady of the House, he slipped out and played with his friends in the yard.

The yard dogs taught him a spring game. It was called Catching Air. They played it by scampering about the yard, yipping and yapping, trying to catch as much of the sweet-tasting spring air as they could.

Figaro was playing this wonderful game—Catching Air—one afternoon, when suddenly he felt a drop of rain on his nose. A moment later the rain came pouring down.

Figaro would have dashed inside at once, but the yard dogs invented a new game right on the spot. They called it Catching Raindrops, and Figaro thought it was the best game of all.

He was busily playing the game, when suddenly he heard the short, very tiny bark that meant his mother wanted him. He whipped around and scampered toward the house—right through all the mud that the rain had made.

Into the house he went, then hurried from room to room in search of his mother. He found her at last in the parlor, where she sat at the feet of the Lady of the House. The Lady, dressed in a beruffled white gown, was smiling as she poured tea for two of her friends.

Figaro guessed that the time had come—when he was to become a lapdog. Before his mother could stop him, he leaped up into the lap of the Lady of the House.

The Lady gasped and put down the teapot with a clatter.

"Oh, my!" she exclaimed. "Look at you, Figaro!" She lifted

Figaro off her lap. "You're wet and muddy!" She gave Figaro a little push, and he ran off and hid under a sofa.

The Lady of the House stood up and inspected herself. She sighed when she saw the muddy paw prints on her lovely white dress. But then she laughed. "Well, we learn something from everything," she said. "This has proved to me that our Figaro is certainly not meant to be a lapdog."

Then the Lady of the House excused herself, saying she would have to change her dress before she served tea.

When she had gone, Figaro's mother called him out from under the sofa and led him into the hall. "How did you ever get so wet and muddy?" she asked quite crossly.

"I was playing with the yard dogs," Figaro whimpered. "The yard dogs are my friends."

"Well," said his mother, "you'll have plenty of chance to play with your friends from now on. Because you are no longer a lapdog, my son. Now you are a yard dog."

She was right. That very day, the Lady of the House had Figaro move out to the kennel to live with the yard dogs.

Figaro, of course, was very happy.

In time, his mother got used to the idea, too. Standing at a back window, she would point him out to the other lapdogs when she saw him playing Catching Leaves or Catching Snow or Catching Air or Catching Raindrops with the dogs in the yard.

"That's my son Figaro," she would say proudly. "He's the best leaf catcher and snow catcher and air catcher and rain catcher of the whole lot."

The Mysterious Egg

"HURRY!" SHOUTED Bobby Bear. "It's almost time!"

It was Easter Sunday afternoon, and all of the little animals in the forest were gathered at the cave where Bobby lived with his father and mother. This was the day of the big Easter egg hunt, and the animals were jumping about excitedly, eager to begin.

It was a perfect day for the hunt. Except for one fat cloud, the sky was so clear that it looked like a big blue mirror. The bees were buzzing about, poking curiously into the new spring flowers. The grass was just high enough to hide an Easter egg.

Mrs. Bear was in charge of the hunt. "Listen, everyone," she called to the little animals. "The Easter Rabbit has told me that he hid the eggs in very difficult places, so finding them will be that much more fun. Now remember, as soon as you see the sun begin to settle to rest, you must all hurry back here. Then we'll see who wins the prizes. . . . Ready, get set, *go.*"

Away the animals darted. Sandy Squirrel and Peter Hedgehog went one way, Billy Beaver and Timothy Deer went another way, and Bobby Bear and Chuck Woodchuck went another.

Bobby Bear and Chuck Woodchuck chose a path that led into a part of the forest where they had never been before.

"The place where you haven't been before is always the most difficult place to look," said Bobby. "And Mother told us that the Easter Rabbit hid the eggs in difficult places. That means we're sure to find the most eggs!"

It certainly seemed as if Bobby were right. Soon he and Chuck found three Easter eggs, one right after the other. One—a blue egg—was hidden inside a hollow log. Another—a pink egg—was hidden in the fork of a fallen limb. And another—a green egg—was hidden in a clump of tall grass.

"Hurrah!" said Bobby. "We're sure to win a prize!"

On they went, into the forest, finding more eggs at every turn of the path. Very soon they had their baskets full of Easter eggs.

"Let's go back now," said Chuck. "I'm sure no one else has found as many eggs as we have."

"Just one more," said Bobby. "As soon as we find one more egg, we'll start back."

So they kept going, getting farther away from the cave with every step. But they didn't find any more eggs.

"I don't think the Easter Rabbit came this far," said Chuck.

"Of course he did," replied Bobby. "You heard what my mother said—he hid the eggs in the most difficult places. And the farther away they are, the more difficult they are to find."

So on they went, looking into hollow logs, looking behind fallen limbs, looking behind big stones, looking into clumps of tall grass, looking everywhere that an Easter egg might be. The farther they went, the thicker the woods became, until finally they came to a place where the trees were so close together that the branches shut out the sun.

"Let's go back," said Chuck worriedly. "I don't like this place—it's too dark."

Bobby felt the same way, but he didn't want to admit it. "Let's have just one more look," he pleaded. "Then we'll turn around and go back."

"It's so dark here, I can hardly see," complained Chuck. "I don't think I could see an egg even if there was one around."

"Here," said Bobby. "Here's a bush. We'll look in the bush, and then we'll—" Bobby stopped. Then he shouted happily, "I've found it! Another egg! It's right here in this bush!"

"Good," said Chuck. "Bring it along, and let's go home."

The two hunters started back, Bobby carrying the new egg with the basketful of other ones he had found. After a while the woods became lighter again, and they stopped to rest.

"Let's see that new egg," said Chuck.

It was easy to tell the new egg from the others. It was small and white, and it was sprinkled with a great number of brown speckles.

"Are you *sure* that's an Easter egg?" asked Chuck.

"It must be," said Bobby. "It certainly was a very difficult one to find."

After they had rested, Bobby and Chuck started out again. Before long the sky began to darken.

"It's that one fat cloud," grumbled Bobby. "It's going to rain on us. We'd better find some shelter for our Easter eggs or they'll get all

wet and the Easter color will wash away."

Bobby and Chuck took cover inside a hollow log—and just in time. The sky grew darker, and then the rain came pouring down.

It was snug and dry inside the log. Bobby sat close to the opening, watching the rain, and Chuck curled up behind him to count his eggs. Suddenly he nudged Bobby. "Don't look now, but I think that new egg just moved!" he whispered.

"Don't be silly!" Bobby whispered back. "You know that eggs don't move!"

"Maybe not," said Chuck, "but—"

Just then, they heard a strange sound coming from somewhere out in the rain.

"Gray-go-reeeeeeee! Gray-go-reeeeee!"

Bobby and Chuck huddled together.

"What is it?" Bobby said, shivering.

"It must be a ghost!" answered Chuck, quivering.

But it wasn't a ghost. A moment later, Bobby and Chuck saw a hen pheasant come stalking out of the dimness. She went right by the hollow log, looking this way and that and calling: "Gray-go-reeeeeee! Gray-go-reeeeeeee!"

They could hear her strange call long after she had disappeared down the path.

"That must be a secret signal," said Bobby.

"What *kind* of a secret signal?" asked Chuck. "Do you think she's a lady robber signaling to her gang?"

"I didn't mean *that* kind of secret signal!" said Bobby. "What I meant was—"

Bobby was interrupted by another strange sound. This one came from the speckled egg.

"Tat-tat-tat!" went the egg.

Bobby and Chuck huddled together again.

"It's a bomb!" wailed Chuck.

"I don't know what it is," said Bobby. "But it isn't a bomb. The Easter Rabbit wouldn't hide a bomb. It's probably some kind of surprise egg."

"It's a surprise to me, all right!" said Chuck. "Let's take it to your mother and find out from her just what kind of a surprise it is!"

That was just what they did. Bobby picked up the new egg, and he and Chuck dashed back to the cave. By the time they got there the rain had stopped and the sun was shining again, and Mrs. Bear and all the other little animals were gathered around waiting.

"We . . . found . . . this . . . egg . . . in . . . the . . . forest," panted Bobby, running up to his mother. "Listen . . . to . . . it!"

"Tat-tat-tat! Tat-tat-tat!" went the egg.

Mrs. Bear began to laugh. "Don't you know what you have there?" she asked.

Before either Bobby or Chuck could answer, there was a very

loud "Tat-tat-tat!" and the egg cracked open. Out stepped a baby pheasant!

At almost the same moment, the hen pheasant whom Bobby and Chuck had seen in the forest came running up.

"My baby!" the pheasant exclaimed. "My little Gregory!"

Bobby and Chuck looked at each other. They knew now that "Gray-go-reeeeeeee!" wasn't a secret signal at all. The mother pheasant had simply been calling her baby—Gregory!

"You bad bear!" the pheasant scolded him. "You stole my baby!"

"I'm sorry to have worried you, Mrs. Pheasant," said Mrs. Bear. "But I'm sure the boys were not aware of what they were doing."

Then she explained that Bobby and Chuck had been on an Easter egg hunt and had mistaken the pheasant egg for one left by the Easter Rabbit.

Mrs. Pheasant understood. And she was so happy to have her baby back that she forgave the boys for taking him from the nest.

Then Mrs. Bear handed out prizes to the hunters. The prize for finding the most eggs went to Sandy Squirrel and Peter Hedgehog. Bobby and Chuck had been in such a hurry to get back to the cave with the mysterious egg that they had left their baskets in the hollow log.

"We also have a prize for the most unusual egg," said Mrs. Bear. "I wonder who should get it."

All the animals laughed. There was no doubt at all in anyone's mind which two hunters had brought back the most unusual egg that day!

Franklin's Upside-Down World

FRANKLIN WAS a sloth. All day long he did slothlike things; that is, he hung around in the trees, breakfasting, lunching, and dining on leaves.

There was nothing very strange in this, and yet all the animals in the jungle thought Franklin was a very odd fellow. The fact was that when he was hanging around in the trees, Franklin always hung *upside down.*

Of course, Franklin didn't think he was upside down. He thought that was the way he was supposed to be. No one had ever told him that he was upside down and the rest of the animals in the world were right side up.

Franklin was quite happy with his life the way it was. Hanging

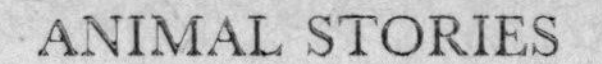

upside down, he ate and slept, then slept and ate, then ate and slept some more. It seemed to him a perfect way to live.

But one day some men came tramping through the jungle. They looked up and saw Franklin hanging upside down from the limb of a tree, just as Franklin looked down and saw them. He thought they looked quite harmless, standing there on their heads, and so he didn't pay much attention to them. He just went on nibbling a leaf.

The men, however, were very excited. They had come into the jungle to look for strange animals to sell to a zoo. Franklin was by far the oddest animal they had yet come across, although they weren't sure what kind of animal he was.

"I think he is a monkey who has lost his tail," said one man.

"I think he is an oversized mouse who has climbed the tree and can't get down," said another.

"I think he is an elephant who shrunk and then, embarrassed at being so small, climbed the tree to hide," said a third.

The one thing they all agreed on was that Franklin belonged in the zoo.

"He can't be very happy, hanging upside down like that," said the leader of the men. "Why, I'll bet he thinks the sky is the ground, and the ground is the sky."

The man was right. Franklin *did* think that the sky was the ground and the ground was the sky. That was the way he saw things. But it didn't mean that he was unhappy. He was very happy being upside down, because he didn't *know* he was upside down.

Very quietly, one of the men climbed the tree with a sack. He slipped the sack over Franklin's head and brought him down to the ground. Franklin paid no attention, for he was still upside down, and so, as far as he was concerned, everything was right side up. Besides, he was too sleepy to care. He immediately dropped off for a nap.

Hours later, however, when Franklin woke up, he was not happy at all. The men had put him into a cage! And, horror of horrors, they had put him in right side up. His feet were on the bottom of the cage.

That would have been fine for any other animal, but not for Franklin. Standing on his feet made him dizzy. He looked around, and he thought that the world had been turned upside down.

Instantly, he shut his eyes, closing out the sight. He hoped that if he didn't look the world would right itself again. But it didn't help. When he opened his eyes and peeked, the world was still topsy-turvy. The sky was where the ground ought to be, and the ground was where the sky ought to be—at least, according to the way Franklin saw it.

One of the men stopped by the cage.

"There, you're much happier now, aren't you?" he said to Franklin. He walked on, certain that he had done Franklin a great favor by putting him on his feet so that Franklin could see the world as he, the man, thought it should be seen.

Well, it was doubtful that Franklin could have answered even if the man had waited. Franklin was so frightened that he couldn't even think, let alone answer silly questions. He stood there in the cage, his teeth chattering, staring bug-eyed at the upside-down world.

Franklin saw another cage. And in it he saw a jaguar who was pacing back and forth, muttering not-very-nice things about men who came along and captured jaguars and shipped them off to a zoo.

Franklin was nearly startled out of his wits. Because, as he saw it, the jaguar was as upside down as he was. The jaguar, according to Franklin's view, was pacing back and forth with his paws in the sky.

"It's the end of the world!" Franklin moaned. "When a jaguar walks in the sky it's surely the end of the world!"

Then he closed his eyes again and vowed that he wouldn't open them until the world had come to its senses.

The next few weeks were very difficult for Franklin. He couldn't eat and he couldn't sleep. The men put leaves in his

cage, but he couldn't touch a bite. His stomach was upset—almost as if it had been turned upside down.

Sometimes the men came and talked outside the cage. He heard them mention a ship. One day his cage was lifted up and put into a dark place, and then, for days, he heard water splashing.

At last the cage was lifted again and put into a truck. And, not long after that, Franklin heard a new voice. It was the voice of a man, but it was different.

"Great heavens!" the voice said. "What have you done?"

Franklin opened his eyes. He saw a man with a beard and very kindly eyes.

"That's a sloth you have there," the bearded man said to the others. "He's supposed to be hanging upside down. Why, poor thing, he probably thinks the world has turned topsy-turvy!"

"Is that so?" said one of the other men, surprised. "We didn't know that. We thought he didn't know which end was up, hanging around by his heels like that."

The man with the beard opened Franklin's cage and took him out. He carried him to another cage. Inside this cage was a tree—a wonderfully leafy tree.

"There you are," the man said to Franklin, hanging him upside down on one of the branches of the tree. "Now, isn't that better?"

It certainly was. The world, according to Franklin, was suddenly right side up again. He was so happy that he remembered that he was hungry. He began nibbling leaves as fast as he could. Soon afterward, he fell into a deep, contented sleep.

Hours later, when Franklin awakened, he opened his eyes v-e-e-e-ry slowly, afraid of what he might see. But he needn't have worried. The world was just as it should be. Outside his cage was a great crowd of people—men and women and happy children. And all of them were standing on their heads, just as they should be.

The Big Bicycle Horn Hunt

SOCRATES AND DILBERT, the Hollywhistle cats, were sunning themselves on the window seat.

"Did you know," said Socrates, "that tigers are our cousins?"

"Not *my* cousins," said Dilbert. "My cousin is the Joneses' cat who lives down the street."

"I don't mean close-by cousins," said Socrates. "But we are all part of the same big family. There was a time, long, long ago, when cats prowled the jungle, just the way tigers do today. We used to hunt for our food instead of having it brought to us."

"I like the way it's done right now," said Dilbert. "I don't think we'd have much luck hunting for a bowl of milk in a jungle."

"Milk!" exclaimed Socrates. "We wouldn't be hunting *milk.* We'd be hunting other animals. And if we had to hunt for our food, we'd get a lot of exercise, and you wouldn't be as fat and lazy as you are." He got to his feet. "As a matter of fact," he said, "that's a good idea. Come along. We're going out and hunt like tigers."

"But there isn't any jungle around here," Dilbert complained.

"There's a vacant lot next door, isn't there?" asked Socrates as they left the house. "That's *almost* like a jungle."

When they reached the vacant lot, Dilbert said, "Look at those high weeds. We'll never be able to find anything in there."

"We have noses, haven't we?" said Socrates. "We'll sniff our food—just the way the tiger does."

Dilbert sniffed. "I smell milk," he said. "Let's go back to the house. Maybe it's lunchtime."

"Don't be a quitter!" Socrates replied. "Follow me. And be very quiet. If our food hears us coming, it might run away."

"One thing about a bowl of milk," Dilbert grumbled, "you don't have to sneak up on it."

Cautiously the two cats crept into the high weeds, with Socrates leading the way.

Suddenly the quiet was broken by a loud SQUAWWWWWK!

"What was that?" Dilbert whispered, trembling.

"A ferocious beast!" replied Socrates. "Don't make a sound! Maybe it won't see us!"

Minutes passed, and all was quiet.

"I guess we can move on now," Socrates said.

But as he stepped forward, the SQUAWWWWWK! sounded again.

This time, however, Dilbert was not the least bit frightened.

He began to snicker. "Just look under your hind feet," he said slyly.

Socrates looked. What he saw was a bicycle horn. Someone had tossed it into the vacant lot, and Socrates had stepped on it!

Dilbert grinned.

"Well, it *sounded* like a ferocious beast," grumbled Socrates. Then he crept forward again, and Dilbert tagged after him.

They hadn't taken more than a few steps when Socrates stopped so suddenly that Dilbert bumped into him.

"Shhh!" he said. "I've found our food. It's asleep in the weeds!"

"What is it?" Dilbert whispered.

"I don't know," replied Socrates. "But it's furry and it has one eye." When Dilbert had crept up beside him, he went on, "Now, you sneak up on it and pounce."

"Why me?" Dilbert protested. "This wasn't my idea."

"You're the one who needs the exercise," Socrates explained.

Nervously, Dilbert got ready to spring.

"Now! Pounce!" said Socrates.

But, instead, Dilbert began to chuckle.

"Quiet!" Socrates whispered. "You'll waken it!"

Dilbert kept on laughing. He laughed so hard that he tumbled over in the weeds. "Look!" he finally managed to say. "Look at your ferocious beast!"

Socrates crept forward—and saw what it was that had made Dilbert laugh so hard. The furry animal wasn't a furry animal—it was a furry house slipper. And the eye wasn't an eye—it was a shiny button.

"From now on," Socrates said crossly, "you go one way and I'll go another. I'd rather hunt alone. And remember," he snapped, "if you see anything, pounce on it!"

So Socrates went one way, and Dilbert went the other.

"Now I'll show what a great hunter I am," Socrates said to himself. He began at once to find things. He found an old rubber boot, and the steering wheel of an automobile, and a doorknob, and a rusty coffeepot—but he did not find any food.

He was about to give up, when all of a sudden he heard a strange sound just ahead. He could not see what was making the sound because the weeds were too high, but he knew that at last he had found an animal. For what he heard was the sound of nibbling.

"I'll go and get Dilbert to help catch him," he thought. But then he decided that if he moved, the mysterious animal might hear him.

"I'll have to do it all myself," he decided.

He drew back, and with a mighty effort he leaped high into the air, aiming for the very middle of the high weeds.

"Oomph!" There was a loud and very familiar groan. Socrates

looked down and discovered that the animal he had pounced on was not so mysterious after all.

It was Dilbert!

"Watch out!" Dilbert exclaimed, struggling to his feet. "You're crushing my strawberries!"

For a moment, Socrates was puzzled. Then he looked around and saw that he had landed in the midst of a patch of wild strawberries. He saw, too, that Dilbert had apparently been there for quite a while. His friend was so stuffed with strawberries that he looked as if he were about to burst.

"Is this what you call hunting?" Socrates scolded him.

Dilbert just smiled. "I did what you told me to do," he said. "You told me that if I found something I should pounce on it. That's what I've been doing—pouncing on these ferocious wild strawberries."

"Oh, well," Socrates sighed. "I guess you're right—it is *wild* food. Maybe you're not such a bad hunter, after all."

"Have a strawberry," said Dilbert.

Socrates did. But, just to prove that he was as good a hunter as Dilbert, he pounced on it before he ate it.

A Jungle Jumble

ONE AFTERNOON a monkey scampered into the clearing where the jungle animals were playing games.

"Run! Run!" he cried. "Run for your lives, everyone!"

The animals stopped their game of leapfrog and stared at the monkey in astonishment.

"The Great Hunter!" the monkey went on, trembling. "He's in the village! He and his helper are preparing nets and traps. They're going to capture all of us and take us to the zoo!"

When they heard that, the other animals began running around in circles in the clearing, bumping into each other a great deal and shrieking, "Run! Run! Run for your lives!"

Fortunately, the lion, who was the king of the jungle, was not quite so easily frightened. As he came ambling along, he gave a mighty roar.

"What is the reason for all this noise?" he demanded.

The monkey explained again that the Great Hunter was in the village and that he and his helper were preparing nets and traps.

"They're going to capture us and take us to the zoo!" said the monkey.

The lion thought about this for a few moments, frowning to himself in a wise and kinglike way.

Then he said, "Since we know that the Great Hunter is here, and since we know what he intends to do, there must be a way to stop him from doing it. All we have to do is think of the way."

The other animals immediately felt much better.

"We can all hide our heads!" said the ostrich. He was a bit silly, and he thought that if his head were hidden and he couldn't see others, then others couldn't see him.

"We must think of something else," said the giraffe. "The Great Hunter might not find my head, but he would surely find the rest of me. And I'd hate to be taken off to the zoo without my head."

Then the monkey made a suggestion. "We could all climb to the very tip-tip top of the trees," he said. "The Great Hunter would never find us there."

"But I can't climb," said the hippopotamus. "I suggest that we all go down to the river and hide under the water."

"That's well and good for you," replied the monkey. "But if I try to hide underwater, I'll drown. If I have a choice, I'd rather be taken off to the zoo than drown."

That's the way it went. Nearly all of the animals offered a solution to the problem, but none of the offerings were of much help.

Then the lion spoke up again. "Suppose—" he said, "suppose the Great Hunter—who is looking for ordinary lions and tigers and giraffes and elephants and so on—suppose he found a girelephant, or a lippopotamus, or a rhinopard."

The other animals looked at the lion as if they could not believe their ears.

"What do you mean?" asked the elephant.

"I will tell you," the lion replied. And when he had explained his idea, the other animals decided that, without a doubt, he deserved to be king, because he was the cleverest of them all.

That night, when the moon was very high, and very round, and very pale, the animals crept up to the edge of the village to put the lion's plan to work. They could see the Great Hunter and his helper putting the nets and traps together for the hunt the next morning.

"Now!" said the lion, signaling to the giraffe and the elephant.

The elephant and the giraffe stepped out of the jungle, side by side, and went strolling along the edge of the village. The elephant tucked his head and trunk down between his front legs, out of sight. And what they looked like—side by side in the moonlight—was an elephant with the head and long neck of a giraffe!

At once there was a shout of excitement from the Great Hunter.

"Look!" he cried to his helper. "There in the moonlight—it's an eight-legged girelephant!"

"Either that or an eight-legged elephaffe!" agreed the helper.

No sooner had the girelephant—or elephaffe—disappeared than another strange-looking animal appeared, silhouetted against the full moon.

This time it was the lion and the hippopotamus side by side. And the hippo had his head down between his front legs, so that, together, the animals looked like a hippopotamus with the great, shaggy head of a lion.

"An eight-legged lippopotamus!" shouted the Great Hunter.

"Either that or an eight-legged hippolion!" agreed the helper.

Next, the rhinoceros and the leopard appeared side by side in the moonlight, with the rhinoceros keeping his head tucked neatly out of view between his front legs.

"An eight-legged rhinopard!" gasped the Great Hunter.

"Either that or an eight-legged leoceros!" agreed the helper.

And so it went, throughout the night. Two by two, side by side, looking like one, the animals passed on parade. And at each strange sight, the Great Hunter became more excited.

At last the moonlight began to fade, and the animals crept back into the jungle. They were delighted with the way the trick had gone.

"I think we've seen the last of the Great Hunter," said the lion. "No hunter who is looking for ordinary lions and tigers and hippopotamuses and giraffes for the zoo would waste his time around here, where there are only lippopotamuses and girelephants and rhinopards."

"That's right," said the rhinoceros. "We're safe at last." Then they all lay down in the clearing to get a little sleep.

They had no sooner dozed off than the monkey came rushing into the clearing once more. Again he was crying, "Run! Run! Run for your lives!"

The other animals awoke and began running around the clearing, bumping into each other and shrieking, "Run! Run! Run for your lives!"

"But why?" demanded the lion. "What has happened?"

"Our trick didn't work," the monkey wailed. "The Great Hunter and his helper are on their way here now, and they're bringing their nets. We're doomed!"

The animals turned to the lion. "What can we do now?" they all asked at once.

The lion looked thoughtful again—though not quite as wise or as kinglike as he had before. "The only thing we can do now," he said sadly, "is tell ourselves that we may like life in the zoo. Because," he added, pointing, "here comes the Great Hunter now!"

Sure enough, the Great Hunter and his helper tramped into the clearing at that very moment, carrying their nets.

The animals huddled together, trembling so hard that the ground trembled with them. The ostrich buried his head and the monkey looked for a tree and the hippopotamus wished he were walking on the river bottom. They all waited for the nets to fall.

But, oddly, that wasn't what happened. Instead of throwing his nets, the Great Hunter and his helper stood in the center of the clearing and looked around disappointedly.

Then the Great Hunter spoke. "Let's not waste our time here," he said to his helper. "These are only ordinary lions and tigers and hippopotamuses and giraffes and such. There's not a lippo-potamus or a girelephant or a rhinopard in sight."

"Right," agreed the helper. "Not a hippolion or an elephaffe or a leoceros anywhere."

"If we're going to find those wonderful new animals for the zoo," said the Great Hunter, "we'll probably have to hunt deeper in the jungle."

"Right," agreed the helper. "Deeper in the jungle."

So, on they went, right past the ordinary animals, without even giving them a second look. And from that day on the Great Hunter and his helper were never seen in that part of the jungle again. For all anyone knows, they are probably *still* looking for the girelephant and the lippopotamus and the rhinopard—or the hippolion and the elephaffe and the leoceros. And they are very, very hard to find.

The House of the Mouse

"I'M ON THE right track!" said Herbert Mouse to himself. "I'm getting close! Just one more minute. . . ."

Herbert was on the trail of something tasty. He couldn't quite make out what it was, but his nose told him that once he found it he was going to have a very fine feast.

Silently, Herbert tracked the smell through the dining room of the house in which he lived, through the kitchen, and into the pantry.

"It's cheese!" he exclaimed in delight. And he was about to take a big bite of his favorite food when a hissing, spitting ball of gray fur leaped out at him from behind a box on the floor.

It was Cicero the cat!

Herbert turned and dashed from the pantry. He ran through the kitchen, through the dining room, straight to the crack in the corner of the hallway.

He just made it. As he slid through the crack that led to his nest in the wall, he heard a swish and a smack behind him. He knew what it was. It was Cicero's paw. And this time the paw had very nearly landed on Herbert!

Safe for the time being, Herbert curled up to rest.

"I'm tired of this kind of life!" he muttered to himself. "I have to go out hunting for every bite of food, and the people who own this house do their best to hide the food where I won't find it."

As he thought about his problems, Herbert became so angry that he trembled. "And that isn't all!" he grumbled to himself. "Every time I stick my nose out of the hole to track down my dinner, that cat pops up and chases me. Is that any kind of a life for a mouse? Nosirree!"

Just outside the crack, Cicero hissed fiercely.

"If you don't go away, I'll move out of this house!" Herbert shouted. He always felt quite brave when he was safe in his nest.

"Meow-ow-ow!" snarled Cicero.

"You'll be sorry," Herbert said. "I'm leaving. I don't need you, and I don't need this house. I'll find a house of my own. A house where there's no cat!"

"Meow-ow-ow!" Cicero snarled again. It was clear that he didn't believe a word of it.

Now Herbert *had* to leave, whether he really wanted to or not. He had to show Cicero that he meant what he said. He slipped out through the other crack in the wall, the one that led through the bricks to the outside of the house, then scampered across the yard and under the fence.

"Hurrah!" he cried joyfully. "What fun I'll have now!"

Then he went off in search of a house of his own.

Before long, Herbert met a sparrow. Herbert told the sparrow that he was looking for a house of his own—a house without a cat—and asked if he knew where he might find one.

"Well, yes, as a matter of fact, I do," the sparrow replied. "At the end of this block there is a vacant house, and, as far as I know, it doesn't belong to anyone."

"Vacant? What does that mean?" Herbert said.

"That means it's empty," the sparrow answered. "There's no one living in it."

"No one? Not one single soul?" Herbert said delightedly. "Why, that's exactly what I'm looking for!"

"However—" the sparrow began.

But Herbert didn't wait to hear any more. He darted off, and soon he was running up the steps of the house at the end of the block.

The old house was very large and quite squeaky. Herbert entered it with care. He could hardly believe that there was really a house that didn't have a cat.

When he reached the dining room, Herbert called out, "Hello there! Cat? Can you hear me?"

There was no answer.

Herbert smiled to himself. Apparently it was true—there was no cat in the house.

"Ah, what a fine and beautiful house," Herbert sighed. "Just the place for a mouse like me. I can live here in peace the rest of my life."

He was so happy that he did a dance around the dining room, feeling perfectly safe for the first time in a long, long while. After that he curled up right in the middle of the living room and took a nap. He could never have done that in the house where he had lived before. Cicero the cat would have been on him in a whisk.

Later, when Herbert awakened, he stretched, then sniffed the air to catch the odor of food. After a good nap, he was always hungry.

He couldn't smell a thing. "I must not be close enough to the pantry," he said to himself.

He left the living room, crossed the dining room, and entered the kitchen. There he smelled something, and his nose took him straight to it. In a corner of the bread box in the pantry he found some dried-up crusts of bread.

"Well, it isn't cheese, but it *is* food," Herbert said to himself. "And at least I can eat it in peace, without being chased all over by a cat."

Herbert had a lunch of dry bread and then returned to the living room. He did another dance to celebrate his new life in his own house. Then he stretched out for another nap. But, since he had just finished one nap, he really wasn't very tired, and so he just lay awake, thinking.

"I am lucky to have a house of my own," he thought. "Of course, there isn't much to do around here. And the food—I really can't say much for the food. But still. . . ."

Finally he dropped off to sleep again.

That night Herbert didn't get a wink of sleep, for, after two naps, he wasn't tired. All night long he prowled around the house, inspecting each of his rooms, one by one. In them he found—nothing. Nothing but emptiness.

By morning he was hungry again, so he went back to the bread box for another meal of dry bread. It tasted even worse than it had the day before. And as he nibbled, Herbert discovered something very strange. He wasn't one bit happy in his very own house!

"Dry bread for breakfast, dry bread for lunch, dry bread for dinner!" he muttered to himself. "And nothing—*nothing*—to do!"

Sadly, Herbert walked up and down the pantry shelves. "I wonder what Cicero is doing right now," he said to himself. "Playing with that ball of yarn of his, probably, and having a fine time. I suppose he has nothing to do but play, now that I'm gone and he doesn't have to chase me anymore."

Then he smiled. "I think I'll slip back to the old house and see if I can find some cheese to go with this dry bread," he decided.

Out of his very own house he ran, down the street to his old home.

When he reached his nest in the wall, he stopped and listened. All was quiet.

Cautiously, Herbert slipped out into the hallway. From there he darted across the dining room, then across the kitchen, into the pantry. He stopped again. He sniffed. He sniffed cheese!

In no time at all Herbert was nibbling away at a cheese. Nothing had ever tasted quite so good before. He was so hungry—and so happy—that he very nearly forgot to jump when suddenly he heard a fierce meow!

"Eeek!" he squeaked. Cicero the cat had missed him by the width of a whisker.

Herbert fled to his nest with Cicero right behind him.

"Ah, me," Herbert said happily as he scooted across the kitchen. "I've missed old Cicero!"

"Oh, my!" he said as he darted across the dining room. "It's good to be back!"

"Goodness gracious!" he exclaimed as he dived into the crack in the wall. "It's nice to have something to do again!"

And when he heard himself say that, Herbert knew he would never go back to the empty house again.

The Last of the Doo-Henny Birds

ONE AUTUMN MORNING Alexander Squirrel was hunting for acorns among the fallen leaves when he came across a most curious-looking little bird.

The bird was huddled down in the leaves as if he were hiding from something. He was pure white, and his neck was like an ostrich's, his head was like that of a goose, and his feet and legs were like a chicken's.

"Excuse me," said Alexander Squirrel. "I don't believe we've met."

"Shhhh!" replied the bird. "I'm hiding from Freddy Fox."

"Freddy?" said Alexander, surprised. "Why are you hiding from Freddy?"

"He wants to have me for dinner," answered the bird. "I'm the last of the doo-henny birds. Freddy thinks that if he has me for dinner he will become famous, and that is true. When he passes by, all the other animals will say, 'There goes Freddy Fox, who had the last of the doo-henny birds for dinner.' "

"I'll hide you from Freddy," Alexander said. "You can come and live with me in my nest in the old oak tree."

"Thank you," said the doo-henny, "but I can't climb."

"Then dig a hole," suggested Alexander.

"I can't dig," answered the doo-henny.

"Well, then, you'd better run—and run fast," said Alexander.

But the doo-henny replied, "I can't do that, either. None of the doo-hennies have ever been able to climb or dig or run and

hide. That's why I'm the *last* of the doo-hennies. All the others have been caught for dinner."

"You're in quite a fix," said Alexander. "And, to tell you the truth, I don't know how to help you."

"Just cover me over with the leaves again," said the doo-henny sadly. "Maybe Freddy Fox won't see me."

"He has a very clever nose," said Alexander. "He'll find you, all right."

"I'd rather not think about it," said the doo-henny, huddling down in the leaves.

Alexander went on his way, looking for acorns. He could not get the doo-henny out of his mind, nor could he think of any way to help.

While searching for acorns, Alexander found many things. He found a boy scout knife that a boy scout had lost, and a golf ball with two little black dots on it that a golfer had lost, and a fingernail file that a lady camper had lost.

But he didn't find any acorns. At last he headed back toward the old oak tree where he had his nest.

Alexander had not gone very far when he came upon Freddy Fox. And Freddy was indeed hunting the doo-henny bird. He was trotting along with his nose to the ground and calling, "Here, little doo-henny. Here, little doo-henny. Come to dinner, little doo-henny."

"Why are you snuffling the ground and calling?" Alexander asked Freddy.

"I'm looking for the last of the doo-hennies," answered Freddy. "I mean to invite him to dinner." Then, with a sly smile, he added, "He is going to be the dinner."

"I suppose you have a good reason for wanting to have the last of the doo-hennies for dinner," said Alexander.

"The best reason in the world," replied Freddy. "It will make me famous. All of the other animals will say, 'There goes Freddy Fox, who had the last of the doo-henny birds for dinner.' "

"Do you know what the doo-henny looks like?" asked Alexander.

"Of course I know what he looks like," replied Freddy. "He is pure white and he has the neck of an ostrich, the head of a goose, and the feet and legs of a chicken."

"He should be easy to find then," said Alexander. "I'll help you look for him."

"All right, you can help," replied Freddy. "But when we find him, he's all mine—understand?"

"Of course," Alexander said politely. And off they went together in search of the doo-henny.

Alexander was very clever. Whenever they got close to the doo-henny's hiding place, he would point in another direction and say, "I think I saw something white over there. It looked like a chicken . . . or maybe a goose . . . or maybe an ostrich."

Then Freddy would go chasing off in whatever direction Alexander had pointed. Naturally, he never found anything. Not a goose or a chicken or an ostrich, and certainly not a doo-henny bird.

After a while, Freddy said, "You're not much help, Alexander. You've had me chasing all over the forest. From now on, I'll go where my nose tells me to go."

As it happened, Freddy's nose told him to go straight to the pile of leaves where the doo-henny was hiding.

Alexander could not bear to watch. He knew that at any moment Freddy might find the last of the doo-henny birds.

Then he had an idea.

"Wait! Wait!" he called, running after Freddy. "I know what you're doing wrong! I know why you haven't been able to find the doo-henny!"

Freddy halted. "All right," he said crossly. "*Why* haven't I found the doo-henny?"

"Because you're looking for a bird that looks like a goose and a chicken and an ostrich, and surely the doo-henny knows you are looking for him," Alexander said. "Now, everybody knows that

when a doo-henny is frightened it curls up in a very little white ball."

"Hmmmmm," said Freddy. "Is that so? Then I should be looking for a little white ball, is that it? Instead of a bird that looks like a chicken and a goose and an ostrich?"

"Exactly," said Alexander.

"But how will I know it's a doo-henny when I find it?" asked Freddy.

"By its eyes," Alexander told him. "It will be looking out for danger. You'll see two tiny round eyes peeking out from the little white ball. In fact," he said, "I think I saw such a little white ball just a few minutes ago. It was over there in those weeds."

"You stay here—I'll look," said Freddy, and he dashed off toward the weeds.

A few seconds later, Freddy returned. In his mouth he was carrying a little white ball with two little black dots on it that looked very much like eyes.

"I found him!" said Freddy happily. "Alexander, you've been a great help to me. I would have gone on looking for a bird that looked like a chicken and a goose and an ostrich."

"I just did what I thought best," replied Alexander.

"Now I'm going to do something for you," said Freddy. "I'm going to let you have the honor of telling all the other animals that I have caught the last of the doo-henny birds."

"Why, thank you," said Alexander, as Freddy trotted off toward his den.

As soon as Freddy was out of sight, Alexander went over to the pile of leaves and told the doo-henny bird he could come out of hiding.

"You're safe now," Alexander told him. "None of the animals will be looking for you. Freddy Fox has told me to tell them all that he has caught the last of the doo-henny birds."

"But won't Freddy still be looking for me?" asked the trembling doo-henny.

"After he's had you for dinner?" said Alexander. "Of course not. He will never look for you again."

And that is how it came about that the doo-henny bird lived happily ever after. He is living now, for all we know, walking about the forest and looking a little like an ostrich, a little like a chicken, and a little like a goose.

And, incidentally, that is also how it came about that Freddy Fox had a golf ball for dinner one night.

A Round Trip to China

"TOMORROW WOULD be a good day to go exploring," said Sandy Squirrel. "Who else wants to go?"

"Why go exploring?" asked Chuck Woodchuck. "After all, every place is the same."

Bobby Bear and Sandy Squirrel stopped in their tracks and stared at him. "Where did you ever hear that?" said Bobby. "How can everywhere in the world be the same?"

"I don't know how," replied Chuck. "But it is. My uncle told me so. He's been all around the world. And when I said I'd like to travel around the world someday, too, he said not to bother because every place is the same."

The three friends walked on, with Bobby and Sandy looking very puzzled.

"Does that mean that China is exactly like here?" asked Sandy.

"I guess so," answered Chuck. "I guess there's a Big Pond and a Big Hill and a you and a me and a Bobby Bear. Except there, I guess, everything is Chinese."

"I don't believe it," said Bobby and Sandy together.

Chuck grinned. "All right then," he said. "Go to China and see." He turned off onto the path that led to his home.

"What do *you* think?" said Sandy to Bobby as they walked on together. "Shall we go to China and see?"

"Right now?" asked Bobby, surprised.

"Not right now. We don't have time right now," said Sandy. "It will probably take us most of the day to get there. We'll have to start early in the morning to get there and look around and be back home in time for dinner."

"All right," said Bobby excitedly. "Let's go. As soon as the sun is up tomorrow morning, let's go to China and see if every place *really* is the same!"

The next morning, when the sun was just peeping over the horizon and the day still looked very much like night, Sandy and Bobby started out on their trip to China.

They headed up the Long Path—the one that all the animals said did not have an end—walking toward the sun. After they had walked for quite a while, Bobby said, "How will we know when we get there?"

"That's easy," answered Sandy. "Things will either look different or the same, that's how. If we are right, things will look different. But if Chuck is right, things will look the same."

"Oh," said Bobby. But he still didn't know how they would know when they got there.

Sandy and Bobby traveled on, heading straight for the sun. Soon they had to stop, for the sun was directly over their heads.

"Where do we go now?" said Bobby gloomily. "We can't climb into the sky after the sun. Besides, I don't think China is up in the sky."

But Sandy wasn't gloomy at all. "It's noon," he said. "That's what it means when the sun is straight up. And if it's noon, that means the day is half gone. And if half the day is gone, and it takes a whole day to get to China and back, then we must be there right now!"

Bobby looked around. "It just looks like the middle of the forest to me," he said.

"And it looks exactly like *our* forest, too," said Sandy. "So maybe Chuck is right. Maybe every place *is* the same."

"I think we ought to go on a little farther," said Bobby. "I'm not sure we're there yet."

The two friends walked on, following the Long Path. And after a while they met a grown-up bear.

"Excuse me," said Sandy to the grown-up bear, "but could you tell us if this is the way to China?"

The bear looked at them strangely for a second. Then he smiled and said, "Well, yes. Since China is on the other side of the world, and the world is round, almost any way you take will lead you to China."

"Thank you," replied Sandy.

When the grown-up bear had gone on, Sandy said to Bobby, "Did you understand what he said?"

Bobby shook his head. "I'll tell you one thing, though," he said. "I think we're in China, all right. Because that bear we just talked to looked like a friend of my father's. He must be the Chinese bear who is the same as my father's friend back home."

"Then Chuck *is* right. Every place *is* the same!" said Sandy.

Bobby nodded. "Shall we go back now?" he said.

"Not yet," replied Sandy. "Let's go on a little farther. Let's make absolutely sure that everything in China looks exactly like everything at home."

On they went.

"Look!" cried Sandy suddenly. "There's the Big Pond!"

"It's the Chinese Big Pond," said Bobby in astonishment. "We must really and truly be in China. Look over there!" he said, pointing. "There's the Chinese Big Hill!"

Sandy gasped. "It looks exactly like our Big Hill!" he said excitedly.

The two friends began to run, pointing out to each other all of the things that looked exactly like things back home. There was a blueberry bush that looked exactly like their own favorite blueberry bush. And a hollow log that looked exactly like their own favorite hollow log. And a climbing tree that looked exactly like their own favorite climbing tree. In fact, everything they saw looked just like everything at home.

"That settles it," said Sandy. "Every single place *is* exactly the same!"

Suddenly, Bobby pointed again. "Look!" he said. "Not only is every *place* the same, but every*body* is the same, too!"

Sandy looked where Bobby was pointing. He saw a cave just like Bobby Bear's cave at home. And in front of the cave there were a mother bear and a father bear who looked exactly like

Bobby's mother and father.

"Wait a minute," said Sandy, suddenly suspicious. "If those two bears are the Chinese bears who look exactly like your mother and father, where is the Chinese bear who looks exactly like you?"

Bobby thought for a second. Then he looked around. "I'm not in the climbing tree," he said. "And I'm not in the hollow log. You're right—where am I?"

"I'll tell you where you are," said Sandy. "You're right here beside me. And that isn't a Chinese mother and father bear—it's *your* mother and father bear. I know something else, too," he said. "I know why they say the Long Path doesn't have an end. It's because it goes in a circle. A circle doesn't have an end, does it?"

Bobby sighed. "You mean we're not in China? You mean we walked all morning in a circle and we're right back home where we started?"

"That's what I mean," answered Sandy.

"Then we've wasted almost the whole day," said Bobby sadly. "And we still don't know if every place is the same."

"No," agreed Sandy. "But we did find out something. Now we know where the Long Path goes. We won't have to wonder about that any longer."

Bobby felt a little better. "Also," he said, "it leaves us something to do tomorrow. We can go to China again. Only next time we'll head in the other direction. It wouldn't be any fun if we'd already been to China today."

Bobby and Sandy agreed to meet again the next morning. Then they scampered off toward home because it was dinner time. And Sandy was as hungry as a squirrel. And Bobby was as hungry as a bear.

The Hunters

PETER NEVER forgot the day Pal came to live with him. It had been raining and Peter was out shooting make-believe crocodiles in the mud puddles, when his father came up behind him and said, "Here's a pal to go hunting with." And he put a tiny red-brown puppy in Peter's arms.

That was how it happened. And nothing was ever the same again, because Peter and Pal were the best of friends. When Peter went to school, Pal waited all day for him to come home. When Peter did come home, he took Pal out for a long walk up and down the streets of the city.

Sometimes they went to the park and rolled and tumbled on the green hills. Sometimes they just walked around three or

four blocks, and Pal sniffed at everything they came upon—the mailboxes, the trash containers, and the poles that held the traffic signals.

When Peter and Pal went walking they always played a game. It was the same game Peter had played before Pal had come to live with him. They pretended they were hunting. Usually they tracked down bears.

Sometimes they cornered the bears in the doorways of stores. Sometimes they chased them up trees. It was all make-believe, of course, but Peter had a plan. He was training Pal for a real bear hunt.

"Can we go to a forest?" he asked his father one day. "Pal is getting tired of make-believe bears, and so am I."

Peter's father laughed. "Pal isn't a hunting dog," he said. "He's a city dog. I don't think he could find his own tail if it weren't tied on behind."

"He's just never had a chance to show you how good he is," Peter said. "Can't we go to the woods someday?"

"Maybe." His mother smiled.

Peter smiled, too. He knew that his mother's "maybe" usually meant "yes."

Not long after that, Peter's father announced that the next Saturday they were going on a picnic. "And perhaps—I'm not making any promises—but *perhaps* we'll find a forest," he said.

Peter jumped for joy. "With potato salad?" he asked.

His mother nodded.

"And a ham bone for Pal?"

His mother nodded again. "I'll do my best for my two hungry hunters," she promised. Then she laughed. "Look at that dog's ears perk up when he hears you say 'ham bone.' "

"The great ham-bone hunter," teased Peter's father.

The next Saturday the whole family got into the car and drove out of the city and into the country. Peter and Pal sat in the backseat and watched out the window all the way. They saw the tall buildings of the city disappear. Then they began to see meadows and trees. Finally the car entered a forest where there were tall trees everywhere.

Peter was so excited he jumped all over the backseat.

"We're going to hunt bears!" he told Pal. "Real bears! Not just make-believe bears—*real* bears!"

The car turned off the road and pulled into a clearing. Peter and Pal were the first ones out!

"All right, you and Pal may go hunting," Peter's mother said. "But don't go far. We'll have lunch soon, and I have your favorite potato salad and Pal's favorite ham bone."

"Arf," said Pal.

"And don't get lost," said Peter's father. "We don't want to

have to go chasing all over the woods for you when it's time to eat."

"We won't get lost," Peter promised. He and Pal dashed into the woods.

After they had gone a little way, Peter stopped. "Now, remember," he told Pal, "this isn't make-believe. We're looking for a real bear. Are you frightened?"

"Arf! Arf!" Pal jumped up and down, trying to show how brave he was.

"Good," said Peter. "Now, you run ahead and track the bear, and I'll be right behind you."

Pal barked a hunting bark and bounded off. Peter raced after him.

"Arf! Arf!" Pal found a vine on the ground and began a tug-of-war with it.

"Pal!" Peter scolded. "That's no way to hunt! You're supposed to sniff the ground and pick up the bear's trail and follow it to his den!"

Pal dropped the vine and looked ashamed. He sniffed the ground. Then he set out with Peter right behind him.

It wasn't long before Pal found an animal. It wasn't a big bear, however. It wasn't even a small bear. It was a squirrel. The squirrel was sitting in the middle of the trail, munching on a nut. Pal was so intent on sniffing that he almost bumped into the squirrel before he saw him.

"Chee-chee-chee!" the squirrel scolded.

"Aaoow!" Pal gave a howl, tucked his tail between his legs, and raced off to hide behind a tree.

Peter groaned. "If you're afraid of a squirrel," he exclaimed, "what are you going to do when you find the bear?"

Pal peeked out from behind the tree. "Arf! Arf!" he barked uneasily.

Then he came out from his hiding place, making a wide circle around the squirrel, and he and Peter started on their way again.

After a while they came to a tree that had deep scratches on its bark. "I'll bet a bear did that," Peter said. "Come on, Pal, we must be getting close to his den!"

Pal didn't even look at the scratches. He tugged at Peter's trouser leg as if to make him turn back.

"No, I *won't* go back!" Peter said crossly. "What's the matter with you, anyway?" He plunged on through the bushes, with Pal trotting wearily along behind.

There were no more scratches. In fact, there was no more path.

"Arf!" Pal barked tiredly, after they had struggled through the brush for a very long time. Peter looked back, and there was his hunting partner lying down on a bed of green moss, his head on his paws.

"Come on," he begged.

Pal wagged his tail but he didn't get up.

"Some hunter *you* are," Peter said. "I suppose you want to give up."

"Arf!" Pal barked again.

"Mom and Dad are going to laugh at you," Peter said. "But if that's what you want. . . ."

The truth was that Peter was tired, too—very tired. "I think we came from that way," he said. "Come on, get up."

They stumbled through the forest in the direction Peter had picked. But soon they slowed and stopped. "No, this isn't the way we came," Peter said. He pointed again. "Maybe that's the way."

But it wasn't. After they had walked awhile, Peter stopped once more. "I think we're lost," he said to Pal.

Pal whimpered and lay down.

Peter sat on a large stone. "I don't know where we are," he said. "We didn't find the bear and now we can't find the picnic. We'll miss lunch."

Pal whined.

"And I'm hungry," Peter said. "Oh, boy, I can almost taste that potato salad! How about you?" He patted Pal's head. "Can you almost taste that ham bone you'd get if we were back in the clearing?"

Pal stood up. He barked. He ran around in circles, sniffing the air. Then he dashed off into the forest.

"Wait!" Peter called, jumping up. "Wait! Wait for me!"

Pal plunged on. And Peter followed, yelling, "Pal! Wait! We're getting more and more lost!"

But that wasn't what was happening at all. For suddenly Peter saw Pal bound into a clearing. And then he saw his mother and father sitting on the grass with the picnic lunch spread out between them.

"Well," Peter's father said as they came running up, "we were getting a little worried. Did you find a bear?"

Peter grinned. "No," he said. "But I did make a discovery. I found out that Pal isn't a bear hunter. He's a ham-bone hunter!"

Then he told his mother and father how he and Pal had been lost, and how Pal had found the way back as soon as he heard the words *ham bone.*

"He sniffed it from way out there," Peter said, "and he tracked it all the way through the woods to here."

Peter's mother and father laughed and said they thought that was very good—for a city dog. And, for a reward, they gave Pal, the ham-bone hunter, his reward right then and there. Can you guess what it was?

The Robin That Didn't Care to Fly

One afternoon when Big Red, the bloodhound, was lying in the backyard with his eyes closed and his nose resting on his front paws, he heard a very small sound nearby. Lazily, Big Red opened one eye, just in time to see a baby robin hop by.

"Hello!" chirped the robin. He hopped over to the sandbox, then hopped up onto the edge of it and stood looking around. After a few moments' rest he hopped down and over to the water sprinkler, where he stopped again to admire the view. Then he hopped past Big Red's nose again, toward the garden hoe that was lying near the entrance to the cellar.

"A hopping robin!" Big Red thought. "Very strange indeed. Why should he hop when it would be so much easier to fly?"

He raised his big head and called over to the bird, "Have you by any chance swallowed a jumping bean?"

The robin hopped back across the lawn and stopped close to Big Red's left front paw. "Hopping is how I get from place to place," he said.

"Always?" asked Big Red.

"Ever since I was born," replied the baby robin. Then he added, "That was not very long ago."

Big Red looked puzzled. "I've never heard of a hopping robin before," said Big Red. "Don't you know that you're supposed to fly sometimes? Didn't your mother teach you that?"

The baby robin looked sad. "I remember her saying something about it," he said. "But soon after I was hatched a great wind blew our nest from the tree, and I have never seen my mother or my brothers and sisters since that day." Then he went on more cheerily, "But I get along well. I learn how to do things very quickly."

"Well," said Big Red with a yawn, "you had better learn to fly." And he closed his eyes, thinking that was the end of the matter.

The baby robin hopped right up to the tip of Big Red's nose. "I don't care to fly," he chirped. "I'm afraid. Whenever I get any higher than the water sprinkler, I feel shivery."

Big Red opened his eyes and smiled. "That's silly," he said. "All the other birds fly, and I've never heard any of them say they were frightened."

The little robin began to shiver. "I'd rather not even talk about it," he said.

"But you *have* to learn to fly," Big Red said gruffly. "You're a bird, and birds fly."

"Why?" asked the robin.

"Why fly?" repeated Big Red, puzzled. "Well, I'm not sure. But there must be a good reason for it."

"All the food is here on the ground," said the robin. "And all the safe resting places are, too. Suppose I flew up into a tree to rest and fell out and injured a wing."

Big Red had to admit that falling out of a tree would be no fun at all. "Still, you have wings," he said, "so there must be a reason for flying."

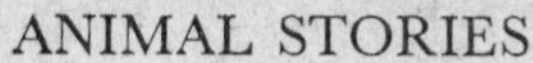

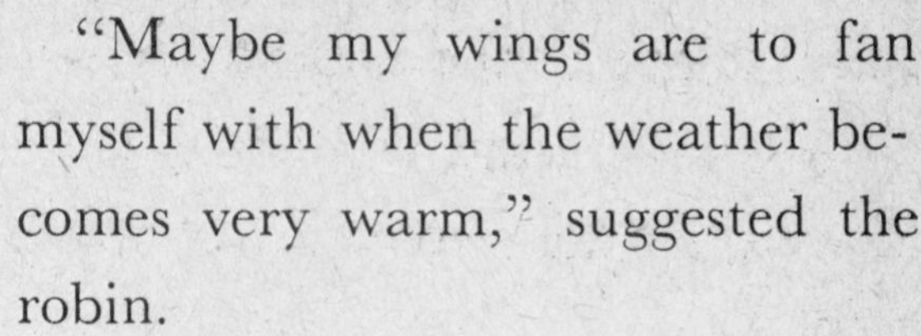

"Maybe my wings are to fan myself with when the weather becomes very warm," suggested the robin.

"What nonsense!" Big Red exclaimed. "You're a bird, and birds are supposed to fly! Now, since you don't have a mother to teach you, I'll do it!"

The robin sighed. "All right," he said. "Fly around the yard once or twice, while I watch to see how it's done."

"Stop that nonsense!" growled Big Red. "I can't fly—I don't have wings. But you do. Now, go over there and hop up on the water sprinkler again. And this time, don't hop down. Fly down."

The baby robin hopped back to the sprinkler and up on its spout. But when he looked down, ready to fly, he shivered so hard that he tumbled off the spout and landed with a thump, right on his beak.

"Maybe we had better start with something closer to the ground," said Big Red. "Hop up on the blade of the hoe and try it from there."

"All right," said the robin patiently, hopping toward the hoe. "But, as I said before, there's no good reason for a bird to learn to fly."

"There has to be a reason," grumbled Big Red. "And if your mother were here, I'm sure she'd tell you what it is."

The robin hopped up onto the hoe.

"Now flap your wings," Big Red called to him.

The robin obeyed. And he reached the ground safely. But it could not be truly said that he had flown, for the distance was very short. Actually, he had hopped down with his wings flapping.

"That won't do," said Big Red. "You can't learn to fly unless you start from a high place. You'll have to get over being afraid." Then he said, "Perhaps if you close your eyes you won't be frightened."

"I won't be able to see where I'm going, either," said the robin. "I'll bump into something and fall to the ground and injure a wing. I tell you, birds were never meant to fly. There's no reason for it."

"All right," Big Red sighed, "keep your eyes open. But tell yourself you're not afraid. Try it from the sprinkler again, and this time keep saying to yourself, 'I am not afraid, I am not afraid.' "

The robin did as he was told.

Big Red smiled. "That's just fine," he said to the robin. "Now flap your wings and fly."

"I can't," said the robin, shivering. "I'm afraid." And just as he said it, he toppled off the spout again and landed on his beak.

At this very moment, Horatio the cat wandered into the yard. He looked at Big Red cautiously, and then he looked at the baby robin.

"What a handsome little fellow!" Horatio purred.

"He may be handsome," muttered Big Red, "but he's not brave. He's afraid to fly!"

Horatio licked his whiskers. "Doesn't fly, you say?" he said, smiling and looking very hungry. "Maybe I can help. Perhaps if I held him in my mouth and ran with him he'd get the idea of how it feels to fly, and he wouldn't be afraid anymore."

"I don't think it will work," said Big Red. "But you can try."

"Remember now," said Horatio, creeping toward the little robin, "this was your idea. If something happens, it will be your fault."

"If *what* happens?" asked Big Red.

"Well, I'll have him in my mouth, and if I happen to swallow, who knows *what* might happen?" grinned Horatio.

While Big Red was thinking about that, the little robin began to hop again. He was shivering a good bit, even though he was not in a high place, for he had noticed that Horatio the cat was getting closer and closer and looking hungrier and hungrier.

Suddenly, Horatio sprang into the air with his paws outstretched to catch the little robin. He almost captured him, but fortunately the robin managed to hop out of the way just in time.

Then began a chase, the little robin hopping frantically in front and Horatio springing after him. They sped around the

sprinkler, through the sandbox, up over the hoe, and around the sprinkler again.

The robin hopped as fast as he could hop, but he could not stay ahead of the big cat. Just as Horatio leaped again, certain of catching the bird this time, the little robin fluttered his wings and flew out of reach. He didn't stop flying until he was perched safely on the branch of a tree.

Big Red was delighted. "You did it!" he said to Horatio. "You taught him how to fly!"

Horatio scowled. He didn't seem at all happy about his success.

From the tree, the robin called down, "Look at me! Look how high I am! And I'm not half as afraid as I was a few seconds ago when I was on the ground."

By that time, Big Red was beginning to understand what had been happening. "I've just figured out what you had in mind," he said. "You intended to have that baby robin for dinner."

Horatio looked insulted. "No such thing," he murmured. "I simply said that I *might* swallow him. Accidents do happen, you know."

Big Red nodded. "Yes," he said, "and now I know why birds have to learn to fly. They have to be able to get away from hungry cats." Then he showed his teeth to Horatio and said, "I also know why cats have four legs—they have to be able to run away from angry dogs."

Horatio did not stay to argue about it. He ran out of the yard and down the street, while overhead the baby robin flew happily from tree to tree.

The Lost Lion

Bobby Bear came rushing into the Bear family cave.

"A dragon! A dragon!" he shouted. "There's a real live dragon out there!"

Bobby's father, who had been taking a nap, leaped up. Bobby's mother, who had been sorting berries, ran and hid her head in the pile of dried leaves that she kept for between-meal snacks.

"What's this? What dragon?" demanded Mr. Bear. "Where is it?"

"Out there!" Bobby panted, pointing toward the door of the cave. "It has more fur on its head than any animal I've ever seen! And it has a little ball of fur at the end of its tail!"

That sounded like a very strange dragon indeed. Mr. Bear

poked his head out the door of the cave to investigate. What he saw was definitely not a dragon; it wasn't snorting smoke. It was, however, unlike any animal he had ever seen.

"I beg your pardon," Mr. Bear said politely. "What kind of animal are you?"

"I'm a lion," the animal answered. Then he said, "Have you seen a little bear around here? I tried to ask him directions and he ran away."

"If you're a lion," said Mr. Bear, "what are you doing in the forest? Lions live in the faraway jungle."

"Not this lion," smiled the lion. "I live in the circus. I've always lived in the circus. I was born in the circus. It's the only life I know."

"That still doesn't explain what you're doing in the forest," said Mr. Bear.

"It's all a sad mistake," replied the lion. "You see, earlier today I noticed the door of my cage had been left a little open. So I went to look for someone to lock it. But as soon as I stepped outside, everyone became very excited and began to run. No one would listen to me. I kept walking and people kept running, and at last I was alone. I'd wandered away from the circus grounds. And now I'm lost."

"I'm afraid I can't help you," said Mr. Bear. "I haven't the foggiest idea where the circus is. But," he said, "you're welcome to stay with us."

"How nice of you," said the lion.

Then Mr. Bear called Mrs. Bear and Bobby out of the cave and explained that their guest was not a dragon; he was only a lost lion.

Soon all the other forest animals began to gather in front of the Bears' cave. They had never seen a lion before.

The lost lion was delighted with all the attention he was getting. He offered to do his trick for his new friends.

"If one of you will get a chair," he said, "and poke it at me, I'll growl at it."

The forest animals thanked him for offering to do his trick. But they didn't have a chair; they didn't even know what a chair was.

"Never mind then," said the lion, a little disappointed. Then he said, "If you don't mind, I've had a hard day and I'm a bit weary. I think I'll turn in for the night—if one of you will show me to my cage."

"Cage?" said Mr. Bear.

"What is a cage?" asked Mr. Squirrel.

"A cage is a place in which to live and sleep," replied the lion, somewhat surprised. "Where do *you* sleep?"

"In a cave," replied Mr. Bear.

"In a tree," said Mr. Squirrel.

The lion shuddered. "I don't think I could sleep very soundly in a tree," he said. "So I suppose the cave will have to do." Then he added, "Although it's not what I'm used to."

The lion slept that night with the Bear family in their cave. But when he awakened the next morning he looked quite grumpy.

"I hardly slept a wink," he said. "The floor is too hard. I'm used to having straw on the floor of my cage." He glanced toward the pile of dried leaves. "If I decide to stay another night," he said, "perhaps I can sleep there."

"Not in *my* between-meal snacks!" said Mrs. Bear crossly.

"Sorry," said the lion. "They look so comfortable. I had no idea that anyone would *eat* them."

Mr. Bear, who wanted to be polite to the visitor, said, "I think we'll all feel better after we've had some breakfast." And then to Mrs. Bear, he said, "Are the berries ready?"

Mrs. Bear brought the breakfast berries.

"Eat as many as you like," Mrs. Bear said to the lion. "The forest is full of them."

But the lion had a very odd look on his face. "Eat *that!*" he said, shuddering again. "It's not what I'm used to. My keeper always brings me a large chunk of raw meat for breakfast. And for lunch and dinner, too."

By now, even Mr. Bear was becoming slightly annoyed. "We eat berries," he said stiffly.

The lion sighed. "Very well," he said. "But it's not what I'm used to."

After breakfast, the Bear family and the lion went out into the sunshine. Immediately, the lion began pacing back and forth in front of the cave entrance.

"What's that for?" asked Mr. Bear, puzzled.

"I haven't the slightest idea," replied the lion. "But this is what I do most of the day. I pace back and forth and back and

forth. It's going to be difficult to do without a cage, of course. I may pace too far one way, or too far the other way, and get lost again."

"Well, we usually play games in the morning," said Mr. Bear. "You're welcome to join us if you wish."

The lion looked uncomfortable again. "I suppose it wouldn't do any harm," he said. "Although it's not what I'm used to."

The game the forest animals played that morning was called Tag. Mr. Bear was chosen to begin. He chased after Mr. Squirrel until he tagged him; then Mr. Squirrel ran after Mrs. Chipmunk until he tagged her; then Mrs. Chipmunk ran after Mrs. Beaver until she tagged her; then Mrs. Beaver ran after the lion until she tagged him; then the lion ran after Mr. Rabbit. But the other animals noticed that the lion had a strange—rather hungry—look in his eye, and that instead of trying to tag Mr. Rabbit, he was snapping his powerful jaws at him.

Mr. Bear called the game to a halt.

"I'm sorry," the lion apologized. "I really didn't mean any harm. You see, I didn't have my raw meat for breakfast, and Mr. Rabbit looked so tasty, and—"

Mr. Rabbit bounded away through the forest without waiting to hear any more. The forest animals decided that it would probably be wise to call a halt to the games for the day.

"Time for morning snacks," said Mrs. Bear, and she began serving the dried leaves.

The lion did not take a snack. "The leaves remind me too much of my nice soft bed back at the circus," he said, "and I certainly wouldn't want to eat my own bed."

The other animals said they understood.

After snacks, the lion offered once more to do his trick for them. "The way it goes," he said, "I enter a very large cage, where a man is waiting with a chair and a whip. He begins poking the chair at me and cracking the whip, and I roar very fiercely." He smiled and added, "Everyone thinks it's a very fine trick."

The forest animals were still not sure what a chair was. But the lion decided that the chair wasn't absolutely necessary. "It's the noise that's important," he said.

Then, to prove it, he opened his great jaws and let out the most astonishing roar that the forest animals had ever heard. It sounded like thunder and lightning and the crash of a falling tree and the roar of a waterfall all rolled into one.

The animals were terribly frightened. They scampered off in all directions, and then, well hidden, they peeked out from behind the trees and bushes at the lion.

The lion looked very disappointed. "That's not what I'm used to," he said.

One by one, the other animals came out of hiding. When they were all assembled again, Mr. Bear said to the lion, "I think I know a way to help you home again."

The lion was delighted. "Not that I don't appreciate your kindness," he said. "But, the fact is, your way is just not what I'm used to."

Mr. Bear led the lion through the forest to the highway that ran along one edge of it.

"Now, just pace back and forth along the highway," said Mr.

Bear. "I will hide behind a tree and we will see what happens."

When the people in the cars saw the lion, they sped away as fast as they could go.

The lion called back to Mr. Bear, "This isn't working! As soon as they see me, they hurry away."

"Just keep pacing," said Mr. Bear.

Not long after that, a truck came along. The truck did not speed past. Instead, it stopped. A man in a white uniform hopped out.

"It's my trainer!" the lion called out to Mr. Bear. "Thank you for helping me. I'm not lost anymore."

When Mr. Bear got back to the Bear family cave he explained to Bobby and Mrs. Bear what had happened. "I knew that the people in one of those cars would tell the circus people where they could find their lion," he said.

Mrs. Bear sighed with relief. "He'll be much happier in the circus," she said.

Mr. Bear winked at Bobby. "And he's not the only one who'll be happier," he said. "A lost lion is just not what we're used to around here."

The Wise Monkey

One day, when Cecil Monkey and the other monkeys were playing leapfrog in a clearing in the jungle, a lion came strolling by. "Look!" chattered Cecil's friends excitedly. "That's Arthur Lion, the wisest animal in all the jungle."

Cecil Monkey noticed something. He noticed that all the other monkeys stopped their game and watched with respect as Arthur walked by.

"I wonder why," Cecil said out loud. "No one stops playing when the elephants and the giraffes and the leopards pass by."

"It's because Arthur Lion is important," one of the other monkeys replied.

"And why is he important?" asked Cecil.

"Because he's wise," the monkey retorted, and he went back to his leapfrog game.

Cecil thought about that for a second. Arthur Lion was noticed because he was important, and he was important because he was wise. Then he said to himself:

"And look at me! I'm a nobody. And why am I a nobody? Because I'm *not* wise, that's why!"

Instantly, Cecil Monkey decided to become wise.

The trouble was, he didn't know exactly how to go about it. He supposed that not playing leapfrog anymore would be a good first step, but he wasn't sure what to do after that.

Finally, Cecil hit on a plan. He would follow Arthur Lion around for a while and discover exactly what he did. By doing exactly the same things, perhaps—perhaps a small monkey could become as wise as a great lion.

Cecil scampered after Arthur Lion and soon caught up with him. Then he put his plan to work. For a while he followed Arthur, and then sometimes he ran ahead and watched him as he approached. In this way, he thought he could find out exactly what it was that made Arthur wise.

After a whole morning of following and peering and studying clues, Cecil decided he knew the secret. The important things, it seemed, were to *look* wise and to give a good deal of advice. He had seen Arthur Lion doing that. Arthur always had a deep, very wise-looking scowl on his face. And every time another animal stopped him and asked for advice, Arthur gave it.

That afternoon Cecil stopped following Arthur Lion and went off on his own. First he found a quiet place in the jungle, where no one could see him. There he practiced making scowly faces.

At first, all he could do was frown. But after a while, with considerable practice, he managed a scowl that was so fierce and so wise-looking that it very nearly cracked his face.

Cecil was so delighted by his success that he grinned—and that, of course, spoiled the scowl. He had to begin all over again. In time, however, he was able to scowl for almost a full minute without breaking into laughter. And when he could do that, he set off to show all the jungle animals how wise and important he was.

The first animal Cecil met along the way was Alphonse Hippopotamus.

"What's the trouble, Cecil?" Alphonse inquired. "You are scowling very strangely."

"This is *not* a strange scowl; this is a wise scowl," Cecil replied. "I have been taking wise lessons. Now, if you have any problems, I will be happy to settle them for you."

"As a matter of fact, I do have one problem," Alphonse said. "I was on my way to talk to Arthur Lion about it. But there's no reason to walk all that distance if I can get the answer from you."

He went on, "My problem is this. I have built a mud slide along the riverbank, but every time I step on it to slide into the water, my feet sink into the mud. I make big holes in the slide, but I don't do any sliding."

Cecil thought for a moment, scowling fiercely. Then he said, "That's a very simple problem. All you have to do is slide down on your back. That will keep your feet out of the mud."

Alphonse Hippopotamus beamed. "That's the best advice I've had today!" he said. And he waddled off to try sliding on his back.

Cecil was so pleased with himself that he came close to grinning again. With an effort, he kept the deep, wise scowl on his face.

At that moment, Mrs. Bush Hen came stalking along the path.

"Good morning, Cecil," she greeted him. "Why are you scowling so strangely?"

"This is not a strange scowl; this is a wise scowl," Cecil replied. "I have been taking wise lessons. Now, if you have any problems, I will be happy to settle them for you."

"Then you're just the one I'm looking for," Mrs. Bush Hen said. "My problem is this. Do you know Abner Elephant? Well, he's a daydreamer. He never watches where he's going. Every time I build a new nest on the ground, Abner comes bumbling along and steps on it. What can I do?"

Cecil didn't hesitate. "Build your nest in a tree," he said.

Mrs. Bush Hen cackled happily. "What a *mar*velous idea! I'll do that!" And off she went to build a new nest right away.

Cecil continued his walk. He hadn't gone very far when he saw Alphonse Hippopotamus stomping angrily along the path toward him.

"How's your slide working out?" Cecil said.

"You and your advice!" Alphonse grumbled. "When I slide down the slide on my back, I get water in my nose. From now on, I'll ask advice from Arthur Lion!" And he stomped on his way.

"Oh, well," Cecil said to himself. "Anyone can make *one* mistake."

He had not gone very far when he saw Mrs. Bush Hen coming toward him. She was complaining loudly, to no one in particular, and she looked very cross.

Cecil tried to slip away without being seen, but Mrs. Bush Hen saw him.

"You and your advice!" she called out. "I'm a ground bird, not a sky bird. When I tried to climb that tree to build a nest, I fell and nearly broke my tail feathers! From now on, I'll ask advice from Arthur Lion!"

Cecil hid behind a big tree and stayed there for a long while. "Two mistakes out of two tries is more than just accident," he said to himself. "I must be doing something wrong."

Finally, he decided that he needed advice, himself. And so, when darkness fell, he went to see Arthur Lion.

"My problem is this," Cecil said to Arthur. "I wanted to be wise and give advice, so I scowled a wise scowl until my face almost cracked. But the advice I gave was all the wrong advice. What did I do wrong?"

Arthur Lion shook his great head. "Your mistake was in thinking that a scowl would make you wise," he said. "It's using your brain that makes you wise."

Cecil sighed sadly. "I should have known it would not be that easy," he said. "I guess I'll never be wise. Because as long as I've had a brain—all my life—I've never learned to use it. It has always seemed like too much trouble."

"Let me ask you a question," Arthur Lion said. "Why did you want to be wise?"

"So I could be important," Cecil replied.

Arthur Lion's scowl disappeared in a broad smile. "Then your problem is solved," he said. "You *are* important."

"I am?" Cecil asked, puzzled.

"Of course," Arthur said. "You're very important to me. If everyone were wise, how would the world know how wise *I* am? If there were no animals who needed advice, what would I do all day? Do you see? Do you see how important you are to me?"

Cecil was so happy he did a flip-flop! He *was* important. He had been, all along!

"Thank you, Arthur Lion!" he called as he swung off through the trees. He was very pleased to learn that he was important, but he was even more pleased about not having to scowl anymore. Scowling made his face hurt.

The Whitman Library of Giant Books

FAVORITE STORIES
A collection of the best-loved tales of childhood, illustrated by Don Bolognese, Betty Fraser, Kelly Oechsli

THE MERRY MOTHER GOOSE
Over 450 Mother Goose Rhymes, illustrated by Ruth Ruhman

THE MAGIC REALM OF FAIRY TALES
Classic fairy tales, illustrated by Leslie Gray, Judy Stang

STORIES OF JESUS
Told by Thea Heinemann, with illustrations by Don Bolognese

ANIMAL STORIES
By William Johnston, with illustrations by Frank Aloise, June Goldsborough